ENDORSEMENTS

"A delicious and delightful story with a large helping of fun and a dash of romance."
~ Jennifer Beckstrand, award-winning author of the Matchmakers of Huckleberry Hill series

"I'm ready to pull up a chair in The Sweet Shop, savor a slice of cinnamon bread, and dig into this juicy mystery."
~ Dana Mentink – award-winning author of the Love Unleashed series

"A delightful story you'll not want to put down until you finish it. You will turn each page and wonder what will happen next. Naomi Miller is a talented and wonderful author, and I can't wait to read more of her stories."
~ Molly Morris Jebber, author of Two Suitors for Anna

"A sweet, fun and intriguing mystery you can really sink your teeth into."
~ Rachel L Miller – author of the Amish romance series: Windy Gap Wishes

PEACH COBBLER MYSTERY

BOOKS BY NAOMI MILLER

AMISH SWEET SHOP MYSTERY

BLUEBERRY CUPCAKE MYSTERY

CHRISTMAS COOKIE MYSTERY

LEMON TART MYSTERY

PUMPKIN PIE MYSTERY

CHOCOLATE TRUFFLE MYSTERY

PEACH COBBLER MYSTERY

AMISH SWEET SHOP ROMANCE

WHITE CHOCOLATE NEW YEAR

(RELEASING WINTER 2018)

CHILDREN'S BOOKS

SOPHIE FINDS A FAMILY

SOPHIE CELEBRATES THANKSGIVING

SOPHIE'S NEW HOME

SOPHIE GOES FOR A RIDE

(RELEASING FALL 2018)

PEACH COBBLER MYSTERY

BY

NAOMI MILLER

To God be the Glory...

GLOSSARY

The German/Dutch dialect spoken by the Amish is not a written language. It is solely dependent on the location and origin of each settlement. The spellings below are approximations.

ach = oh
aenti = aunt
allrecht = all right
appeditlich = delicious
bopli/boplin = baby/babies
bruder/bruders = brother/brothers
buwe/buwes = boy/boys
danki = thank you
Dat = dad
dochder = daughter
du bischt daheem = you're home
Englischer = non-Amish person
freind/freinden = friend/friends

frau = wife

froh = happy

Gott = God

Gudemariye = Good morning

gut = good

hochmut = pride

hungrich = hungry

in lieb = in love

jah = yes

kaffe = coffee

kapp = cap

kinner = children

kumme = come

maedel/maedels = girl/girls

Mamm = mom

naerfich = *nervous*

nee = no

onkel = uncle

rumschpringe = running around time for youth

schweschder/schweschders = sister/sisters

verrickt = crazy

Was iss letz = What's wrong

wunderbaar = wonderful

A NOTE FROM NAOMI MILLER

Peach Cobbler Mystery was the hardest story I've ever written because it deals with something that should never happen in real life, yet it does. . . and all too frequently.

I must warn you that this is one story that might cause more than a little of the heart-pounding, stomach-clinching reactions that I try so hard to avoid.

Although I aim for stories that are fun to read, full of love, joy, compassion, forgiveness, friendship. . . this is a story that needs to be told.

I didn't want to write this specific story about Bella and her past. As a matter of fact, I kept trying to make her a young widow, but

God had other plans for my writing.

I love the characters and situations found in the Amish Sweet Shop Mystery series and I hope that readers will continue to enjoy reading about Katie and all of her friends and neighbors found in this series.

As with any work of fiction, I've taken license in some areas of research as a means of creating circumstances necessary to my characters or plot. I've created fictional characters in a fictional town. Any inaccuracies portrayed in this book are completely due to fictional license.

God bless you!

~Naomi

... choose you this day whom ye will serve
... as for me and my house,
we will serve the Lord.

Joshua 24:15

For Macy

—— ONE ——

Friday morning began the same as most Fridays had lately, with Katie driving in to work with her *Englisch* boyfriend. She loved starting the day with Travis, who would usually regale her with stories of his family.

"And Bobby declared that he was getting older and wants to be called 'Bob' from now on. Gwen told him he would always be Bobby to her." Travis grinned as he shared the tale with her.

"Bobby yelled and smacked his hand on the table, rattling the dishes. I thought Mom would get upset, but when I looked over at her, she was smiling." Travis chuckled. "Then Bobby told her she can call him Bobby at home, as long as she called him Bob at school."

Katie laughed at his expression, and Travis shook his head a little before continuing. "Of course, then Bobby got angry and ran outside when Sam and Trevor started laughing."

"For sure and for certain." Katie smiled as she thought of her own *bruders*. "That's so cute! I don't remember Ervin, Noah or Caleb ever doing that. Of course, their names are harder to shorten. And we have always used their legal names." Katie laughed, then she asked, "Is Bobby's legal name Bob, then?"

"No, it's not Bob. And it's not Robert." Travis answered, laughing. "His legal name actually is Bobby."

Katie's laughter mixed with his.

"Oh my goodness. I would never have guessed. I always thought Bobby was a nickname." Katie said with a smile. She loved how easily they could talk about family, life at home, their work and people they knew.

"He can use Bob as a nickname, but I think he's gonna need to get over being called Bobby." Travis looked thoughtful. "I guess Mom needs to show him his birth certificate and explain it to him before there's any trouble."

"By the way, how is your *mamm?* With Gwen working at the bakery part time, your *mamm* is doing most of the work at home. Is everything working out *allrecht?*"

"Oh yeah, my *mamm* is doing great! She's fully recovered from the pneumonia and she seems to have more energy nowadays than I can remember her having in a long time. Of course, she misses Dad. . . we all do. . . but it's much easier than it used to be." Travis squeezed her hand, seeming to draw support from her fingers gripping his.

"Hey Travis, I kinda wanted to talk to you about something else before we get to the bakery." Katie hesitated before continuing. "It's about Gwen."

"What about her?" Travis looked puzzled. "Is she not working out at the bakery? Is she not doing her job well enough or something? What's the problem?" His voice held a fierceness that surprised her; she was reminded of a long ago *nacht* when young Gwen had shown up at a singing with a group of older *maedels* who were dressed much too mature for their age.

Especially given that they were at a singing with the plain folk in the community.

"*Nee,* it's nothing like that." Katie reassured him. "It's just. . . she's been very quiet lately.

More quiet than I've ever seen her be. You know how she is. . . normally, she talks and talks and talks. But lately she comes in, does her work and leaves, without hardly saying a word to anyone."

Katie waited a few moments to collect her thoughts, then dove back in. "Is she acting differently at home? Have you noticed anything different about her?"

"Gosh, I don't know. Honestly, I've been spending more time with you, and working more hours at the cafe, so I guess I haven't spent as much time at home as I used to. As far as her job at the bakery, I just figured she was working out fine."

"She *is* working out fine, Travis. But I'm not talking about work. I'm talking about Gwen. . . her personal life. . . her feelings." Katie thought of the young *maedel* who had latched on to her so strongly. It could not be an easy thing. . . to be the only young woman in a house full of men and *buwes*.

"Okay, I'll see what I can find out, if I can without getting her upset. Some days she gets upset at the smallest thing."

"That's a *girl* thing." Katie smiled to herself for the usage of his own language in the popular phrase. "I am surprised that you haven't noticed that I do the same thing at times." Katie smiled again, but said nothing else, not certain they were ready to speak of such deeply personal issues.

"Well, maybe I have noticed a few times, but I thought maybe you were really busy, or having a rough time with your parents or the church leaders. I figured if you wanted me to know about it, you'd say something. I didn't want to ask, in case you didn't want to talk about it or it made you sad. . . or upset."

Katie nodded absently as Travis pulled into the parking lot of the bakery, her mind still very much on his *schweschder*. After he turned off the engine, Katie took his hand, hoping *Gott* would give her the words to say.

"But back to Gwen. . . it may be nothing to worry about, but I just have a feeling about it. When you pick her up this morning, don't ask her what's wrong; just talk to her. See if you can find out if she's having a problem at school, or something at home that you don't know about. I don't know what it could be. I just know she is not acting herself and I am more than a bit concerned."

"Okay, I'll talk to her. But for the next few minutes I want to concentrate on my girlfriend." Travis winked at her. "Are you sure you want to go in the front door. Parking around back we will have a little more privacy."

A light shiver rushed through Katie at the memory. With a building between them and the street and little to no chance of anyone seeing them, she and Travis had gotten more than a little caught up in their goodbyes.

"*Ach*, I am sure. The one time we parked around back, you were late picking up your sister for school." She reminded him.

"You're right." Travis agreed, but the smile on his handsome face told her he was not one bit sorry about it. "I know you're right. And yeah, I forget all about the time when I'm kissing you." Travis leaned over, planting a quick kiss on her lips before she could evade him. He smiled at her, then kissed her again before moving back. "Okay, let me take you inside and then I'll go pick up Gwen and the boys."

Katie laughed at the exaggerated sound of suffering in his voice. As he walked around the front of his car, she wondered if it were something that only *Englischer buwes* did or if all teenage *buwes* acted as if they were pained by the least separation from their girlfriend.

When Travis opened her door with a flourish, she smiled up at him and took the hand he offered to help her from the low vehicle. She loved how Travis always came around and opened her car door, then escorted her into the bakery.

She had considered telling him she had opened up the bakery for years without his help, but she enjoyed the extra time with him and the great care that he showed her. And it did not hurt one bit to hear him tell her how difficult it was for him to leave her.

She never told him that it was easier for her because she was so busy after he left each morning, that she barely noticed his absence.

But, if she were being totally honest, she had to admit she also felt better walking into the bakery with him by her side. Even though everything had worked out fine the one morning she had opened the door to a mess and an obvious theft, knowing everything was safe inside before he left made it much easier to open up each morning.

Knowing she needed to get to her baking before the others arrived, Travis always tried to be respectful of her job duties and to not take up too much of her time while at work. Once he had checked around the bakery, he turned to her.

"I'm glad you were ready to leave earlier than usual. Now for a proper goodbye, Miss Chupp." Travis smiled at Katie, before pulling her into his arms.

They shared a few kisses and Travis did try to keep the time in mind. She had to get to work and he had to pick up Gwen and his brothers, but all of that just seemed to fly out of his head when he had Katie in his arms.

After what felt like only a few seconds to him, Katie pulled away, swatting at him playfully. "Travis, you are going to be late again."

"I don't care." He pulled her back to him and kissed her again. She gave in for a few more seconds before pulling away again, putting a hand on his chest and shoving lightly; it was no delicate little push either. His Katie was no delicate flower. All the stirring and rolling and whipping must really build up her muscles.

He laughed as she pushed against his attempt to pull her against him again. "Can I help it if your kisses make it difficult to leave you?"

When she only laughed, Travis twirled her around and planted a quick kiss on her cheek before spinning her away from him with a laugh of his own. "I will be back soon. Lock up behind me, Katie-girl."

"*Jah,* I will. Then I have a long list of baking to get started on." Katie laughed again and waved as he went out the front door and headed to his car.

Locking the door, she turned towards the kitchen, taking a moment to lean against the counter. She did not want to admit to him just how his kisses affected her, but there were times she wanted to go right on kissing him forever.

It was those times that worried her. They were both much too young to be thinking of a thing like marriage. *Especially with him not being plain.*

And they were both much too old to be taking chances with being alone with nothing but their passion for each other. She had heard stories of what could happen when a *buwe* and *maedel* let themselves get carried away by passion.

Shaking the thoughts away, she pushed away from the counter and headed toward the kitchen, thinking a hot cup of *kaffe* might help to clear her head before she started her baking.

— TWO —

Katie looked up when Freida walked into the kitchen with a swish of the swinging door. "I don't know what to think anymore. I was sure that Bella, or at least Mrs. Mueller, would say something about the father. . . or what happened. But I've learned nothing. . . nothing at all." Freida sounded put out by the lack of information.

Katie nodded at her *freind*. Lately, Bella had

been on everyone's mind. Since her unexpected news, at least to most of the community, about expecting a baby, Katie and Freida had both been watching for the baby's father to show up.

Whenever Freida dropped by, she would chat with Bella or Gwen for a few minutes before heading into the kitchen for a long chat with Katie. And lately it had mostly been about how frustrated she was to be out of the loop about Bella.

Katie sighed before answering Freida. *"Jah.* I know we shouldn't ask her about it, but it is such a puzzle. She has been here almost seven months and we hardly know anything more about her than we did the day she started working here." Katie shrugged before adding. "And I do not know how we can find out anything without offending her."

"I just wish she would talk to us about it." Freida picked up a peach that Katie had discarded and bit into it, chewing thoughtfully for a minute before going on. "I mean, what happened eight or so months ago? Why did she leave everything and everybody she knew and move here, where she didn't know anybody?"

Freida was getting worked up now. "And where is the father of her baby? Why hasn't he shown up here? What is going to happen when the baby is born?"

"Shh. Do not get too loud, Freida. Maybe we should not be talking about Bella when she's in the other room." Katie glanced over in the direction of the swinging double doors, halfway expecting to see Bella push through them and catch them talking about her.

"*Allrecht,* Katie. I will be quiet, but I won't stop talking." Freida seemed determined. "What do you think. . . really think. . . about it?"

"Honestly, I do not know what to think, Freida. All I can think to do is pray. I have prayed that *Gott* will guide her thoughts and decisions, whatever those may need to be." She shrugged again and then continued. "I can only hope that Bella will listen. . . and make wise decisions in the next few months, but I have no idea if she will ever confide in you or me." Katie paused for a moment before going on.

"If she has told Mrs. O'Neal or Mrs. Mueller or anyone else in Abbott Creek anything about her situation, no one has said anything to me and I've not heard one single bit of gossip."

"And what do you think about her living all this time with Mrs. Mueller? Why hasn't Mrs. Mueller said anything about her to anyone?" She looked over her shoulder and then, when she turned back, Freida did lower her voice. "This is the strangest thing to happen here in a long time. It might even BE the strangest thing to happen here."

And then, only a moment later, she paused

and placed a hand on top of her baby mound and when she spoke again, it was as if she had completely forgotten their previous subject. "Do you have any more peach cobbler?"

Laughing, Katie walked over to the big cooler. Pulling out a large rectangular cake pan, she placed it on the counter in front of Freida before taking bowls and spoons out of a nearby cabinet. "Go on. Help yourself. Since both you and Bella have been craving peach cobbler, I try to make certain I have some on hand every day."

Freida smiled as she dished out large helpings of the cobbler into two bowls. "I will be right back."

She went through the swinging doors, but came back into the kitchen in less than a minute with Bella in tow. "Come on, Bella, there's no one out there right now. Take a break. I'll help you listen for customers."

Pushing Bella towards one of the padded

stools, Freida placed a bowl in front of her. "Here. Have some *appeditlich* peach cobbler. You need to get off your feet for a minute or two anyway."

"Umm. Yummy peaches. You know, I used to think women didn't really get cravings; they just wanted attention. But now I know that cravings are real."

Katie smothered a laugh as Freida nodded, her mouth full of cobbler.

Bella, seemingly oblivious to Katie's amusement, went on, her tone very serious. "That book the doctor gave me says women crave food that have nutrients that they need, like iron or potassium." She looked down at the full bowl in front of her, scooping up a large spoon full of the thick cobbler.

"I haven't figured out what nutrients are in peach cobbler that makes my body crave it, but I crave it. All the time." Bella took a large bite of the cobbler. "Oh, we forgot the vanilla ice cream!"

"*Jah,* you did." Katie smiled, then walked back over to the cooler to pull out the container of ice cream. She added a scoop to each of the two dishes. "I wonder if you are both needing something in the peaches. . . or perhaps it's the milk in the ice cream."

"I crave ice cream a lot, too. But even when we don't have ice cream, I crave peach cobbler. I think it must be something in the peaches." Freida remarked.

Katie noticed Bella nodding her head in agreement. "And fish. . . I crave fish almost every day. I looked it up and it could be the iodine. The only other way people usually get iodine is in table salt. . . and most people use sea salt now. It doesn't have iodine."

Katie just watched as Bella talked, surprised to hear so much from her. Usually she was not so talkative.

"Mrs. Mueller bought a big round box of iodized salt and she keeps a salt shaker filled with it on the table just for me."

"That is very considerate of her." Katie replied, thinking of the Mrs. Mueller she had known for years. The person she was now did not fit the memories she had of the woman she had known for most of her life.

"We use iodized salt now, too." Freida said. "So I get plenty of iodine. I do enjoy fish, but I don't crave it all that much."

Watching her get up to carry her dishes to the sink, Katie thought perhaps Bella looked more than a little uncomfortable.

"Bella, how are you feeling?" She watched the young woman struggle to get back on the stool, then give up after a minute and lean against the counter.

"When did you say your due date is?"

Bella looked up toward the ceiling with an expression that reminded Katie of one that she had seen on Freida's face when she was doing difficult mathematics.

"Well, I think it is still a month or so away. I may never know for sure when the doctor counts everything in weeks. Why?"

"I wonder that you should still be working."

"For sure and for certain you should be on your feet less." Freida added quickly. "I have until September, but to hear Thomas, you would think I am going to give birth any moment." She laughed as she scooped up another bite of cobbler.

Bella waved a hand dismissively. "I think I still have plenty of time until I need to stop working."

"Plenty of time! No, you don't!" Freida almost shouted.

"Freida, hush. Don't scare away our

customers." Katie looked over at Bella. "Freida has a point though. It sounds to me like you don't have much time at all. Besides which, are you not going to take some time off to rest and get ready for your baby's arrival?"

"Nah, I feel fine." Bella looked down at her large, round belly, a curious expression on her face. "I don't need to take a lot of time off until after the baby comes."

Freida laughed. "If you had a husband like my Thomas, I am sure he would have something different to say about it."

At the gasp Bella let out, Katie looked at her *friend,* surprised that Freida would go so far.

But Freida had clearly already realized her mistake. A deep shade of red was rapidly spreading from her ears to her nose.

"Bella. . ."

But Bella held up a hand. "It's fine, Freida. I'm good. You're good. It's all good."

"No, please." Freida took Bella's hand in hers. "My mouth gets me into trouble all the time. Just ask Katie." She shook her head, looking down at the floor between them. "I had no right. . ."

Bella interrupted her. "Really, Freida, I'm fine."

But Freida insisted. "Can you ever forgive me?"

Bella let out a breath and finally looked up at Freida. "Of course I can, Freida. I really mean it. It may not seem like it, but I am fine." She squeezed Freida's hand and then smiled.

When she let go, Freida pulled Bella into a hug. Katie looked back and forth between the two women, breathing a sigh of relief. And then she was stifling a laugh, as she realized how funny the picture in front of her was, with the two women's tummies pushing them apart.

Determined not to ruin the moment, Katie

turned her attention to her work. She was already a bit behind schedule anyway. While Freida and Bella hugged, and then started chatting about *boplin* and quilts and clothes, she rolled out dough for sugar cookies.

Freida told Bella about the bassinet Thomas had made and the *wunderbaar* quilt she and her *mamm* had made for the *bopli* already. And when she spoke of all the different colors they had used, Bella spoke up.

"But wait, Freida. Do you not know if you're having a boy or a girl? The doctor told me months ago that I was having a girl."

"Well, we are not seeing a regular doctor, Bella. Thomas and I want to have our baby at home. A midwife from the community will deliver it. And she does not have that sort of equipment."

"Oh." When Bella answered, Katie wondered if she was imagining that Freida actually looked a little disappointed. "Is that safe?" Bella looked concerned.

"*Jah,* Amish *mamms* have been having their *boplin* at home for hundreds of years. The only time they go to the hospital is if there is a problem during delivery, or when there are special circumstances." Freida looked mostly calm as she spoke. "And everything looks to be fine with the *bopli*. The midwife doesn't expect any problems."

"You are much braver than me. I want to be surrounded by doctors and nurses who know just what to do. Especially since I have no idea what to expect."

"What do you mean?" Katie asked.

"Well, I've read the books, but otherwise I don't know what happens. I've never seen anything being born. Not even puppies or kittens. All I know is what the books say about it." She looked down at the floor with her next words. "And to me, it all sounds very complicated and dangerous."

"Oh Bella, the whole thing is completely natural. There's nothing scary about it. You should talk to our midwife." Freida took Bella's hands in hers. "She can answer any questions you have and explain the whole process to you. She would probably even offer to take you with her on a delivery, so you could experience it for yourself. I would have asked her if I had known, but you have been so quiet about everything. We haven't wanted to ask you anything about. . . well, anything." Freida reached over to pat Bella's arm.

"I don't know if I want to watch someone else giving birth. It sounds much too personal." Bella shook her head. "But maybe she could answer a few questions I have."

"Sure. I will go by and see her on my way home. Before I go, is there anything else you want to talk about. . . with us?" Freida looked hopeful, but whatever it was that had made Bella open up even a little was gone.

"I'd better get back out front. I need to check the supplies. A customer might come in soon." And before anything else could be said, she hurried through the swinging doors.

"Well, I guess we're not going to learn anything about it today." Freida shrugged, looking resigned. Then she smiled, "I'd love to take some peach cobbler with me. I might get another craving later on."

Katie laughed. "*Allrecht*. I'll fix you a take-out box, to have later, just in case."

"*Danki,* Katie. What would I do without you!"

After Freida had said her goodbyes and left with her box of peach cobbler, Katie hurried to check her list to see what else needed to be done for the day.

Before she had even finished looking it over, the back door opened. When Travis walked in, Katie was thankful she had continued to work while Frieda was visiting; otherwise, she would never get done on time.

"Hiya, Katie-girl." Travis came over for a quick kiss before walking over to the clipboard on the wall next to the cooler. Checking it, he whistled. "Whew! People sure love your baking. I'll take one load, then come back for the rest. I don't see how you keep up with all these orders. You're amazing!" He winked at her, then headed into the cooler to pick up the boxes ready for delivery.

Katie blushed at his compliments, thankful that there was no one in the kitchen to witness her embarrassment. But secretly, she loved it whenever Travis complimented her.

—————THREE—————

Katie woke early Saturday morning. She bounced out of bed and rushed to the window to open her bright yellow curtains. There were hints of light creeping over the low hills in the distance and the bright promise of a beautiful day lifted her spirits even higher.

She stood at the window and prayed silently for several minutes before padding down the hall to the upstairs bathroom, laughing quietly when she discovered she had to wait for her turn. Even working at a bakery, she was usually not up before her *bruders,* who had the farm to tend to.

Once her hair had been brushed and pinned back, she moved back to her room and dressed in one of her plain, sturdy dresses, then pulled out several things for later.

Travis had asked her last weekend if they could spend this afternoon and evening together. She was looking forward to it and she planned to change into nice, clean clothes after work.

When she had mentioned it to Mrs. O'Neal, her boss had smiled, telling Katie that she might consider taking time off more often to be with her *fella.*

Katie had only nodded. She had not yet been able to give voice to her thoughts on spending even more time with Travis, but she hoped to find the time to speak with him about it soon.

Looking at the small clock on her wall, she

realized he would be picking her up soon so she put her change of clothes in a small bag and hurried to get downstairs.

Since she was taking off at noon, Katie wanted to arrive early so she would have plenty of time to get all the baking done that was needed today. She hoped to be finished with the baking around eleven, but it would take her close to an hour afterward to clean and straighten the kitchen area to make certain it was prepped for Monday morning.

Travis had already said he would be done by noon, and she wanted to be ready for their adventure. He had told her it might be pretty late when he brought her back home, but he hadn't been specific about any of his plans and Katie was more than a bit curious about them.

What sort of plans would he make, she wondered. *And why would he not tell me anything about them.*

She whispered a short prayer while she pulled her shoes on and went out the back door and down the steps to the gravel drive.

Dear Gott, I know that I can trust Travis, but this is still all so new. . . so please guide him in his plans. Keep us both safe and help us to follow your leading . . and to be a blessing to others we might meet today.

Travis woke early, excited about spending most of the day with Katie. Aside from a few hours at the cafe, he would be spending the whole day with her.

While he showered and dressed, he thought about his plans for the day. He knew his plans were pretty simple, but he didn't want to make a lot of fancy plans and spend a lot of money that he couldn't afford. And he knew Katie wouldn't prefer that, either.

Most of the time, it didn't matter what they did, he just enjoyed spending time with her. And, as much as he enjoyed the time they spent surrounded by friends and family, he liked to occasionally have her all to himself. *It will be nice to spend some time with Katie, without family or friends around.*

He thought about how often Bobby or Gwen would tag along with them. . . or Katie would bring along one of her brothers or sisters. *We don't get off to ourselves often enough.*

It wasn't that he minded so much having other people around. It was just nice to spend time with Katie. . . with no one else around.

Whenever they did find time to go off alone, he liked that they would share things about their past. . . and about their future. Travis felt like he was finally getting to know Katie better. In the beginning she had been reluctant to tell him much about her faith and the church and all the things that had made her who she was.

But during the past few weeks, she had opened up about all of that. Of course, the more she told him, the more Travis fretted over Katie changing her mind about being involved with him. He hated the idea of taking her away from her church, and possibly her family and friends. She had said that her family might be a little unhappy with her if she did not join, but that she would not be shunned so long as she did not join, be baptized, and then leave.

Knowing how families who were not Amish could be about cutting people out of their lives, Travis felt his worry was completely justified, but Katie continued to reassure him that she had made the right decision. . . . one that brought them together as a couple, even if it kept her from being baptized or joining the church that her family belonged to.

Shaking off the negative feelings, Travis thought about the plans he had made. Plans that included a long drive, then perhaps a movie and a nice supper at one of his and Katie's favorite restaurants. Then they would have the long drive back to Katie's house, where he would likely be invited in to spend time with her, most likely in the living room or the kitchen.

This was the way of the Amish families in their community. Most often the parents and other siblings went to bed and the courting couple would spend time getting to know one another.

Most nights the courting consisted of a long drive. Since he wasn't Amish, instead of using a courting buggy, the long drives would be taken in his car.

Jake Yoder had offered him the use of a horse and courting buggy, but when he mentioned it, Katie said she preferred riding in his car, so that's what they would do. . . especially tonight.

And usually, on those long drives, they would talk. More and more lately, those talks included discussing plans for the future, which tended to bring his worry to the surface.

Katie would always calm his fears about her not joining the church. . . although he knew her family still had hopes that she was experiencing what they called *rumschpringe,* the running around time for their youth, and that she would eventually return to the faith of her parents.

Thinking about time reminded Travis that Katie wanted to get to work early, so he quickly finished getting dressed and rushed out without taking time for breakfast. Although he was in a hurry to get there, he was always careful to drive slowly, since there were usually buggies on the road, and buggy accidents were something to be avoided at all cost.

It wasn't long before he was pulling in to the Chupp's driveway. Sure enough, Katie was already outside, watching for him. At her feet was a canvas bag.

Turning off the motor, Travis hurried around to open the car door for Katie. He enjoyed doing little things for her, like opening doors, helping her with her coat and always putting her first.

"Good morning, sweetheart. Sorry if I kept you waiting." After waiting for her to fasten her seatbelt, he leaned in for a quick kiss, before closing the door and coming back around to the other side. Once he was in and had buckled his seatbelt, he started the car and soon they were on their way.

"You were not late; you were early, but I was up earlier than I planned. With everything going on today, I just couldn't stay in bed, so I got dressed and came out to the porch to watch for you." Katie blushed prettily. Travis loved seeing the color that reminded him so much of a pink rose filling her cheeks, making her prettier than ever.

"Is everything still okay with our plan for today?"

"*Jah,* I told my parents last night that I had made plans and not to expect me for supper. I could tell they were wanting to ask where I was going, but they said *allrecht* and no questions were asked."

"Good. And you should be ready to leave by noon, right?" Or do you need more time?"

"*Nee,* Mrs. O'Neal told me yesterday that there were no more special orders taken, so it should be just a normal day. I'll be waiting for you at noon. Do you need more time? If you do, it's okay. I can find something to do until you're free."

"Nope. I have permission to leave early at the cafe. I'll be done by 11am. Then I'll run by the bakery and pick up anything that needs to be delivered. Mrs. O'Neal told me yesterday that there were only three deliveries to be made, and an hour should be more than enough time to take care of them."

He looked over at Katie, excited again, thinking of his plans for the day. "Then I'll run back and pick you up and we'll be on our way."

"On our way. . . on our way to where? Are you still determined to keep our destination a surprise?" Katie asked, teasing him.

"Yep, I sure am." Travis grinned. "Actually, Katie, it's not really anything special. At least most people wouldn't think so. It's just spending the evening with you that makes it special."

"I know what you mean. I was thrilled when we began courting, but now, after months of being together and getting to know you better, it's even more special." That same pretty pink color spread over her cheeks again. "It makes me wonder how people grow tired of one another and, even worse, go in search of other people."

"Yeah, that has never made sense to me, either. I mean, I would never get tired of my family. Why would I get tired of someone else that I love? I tell you, sometimes people make no sense at all."

Travis pulled into the parking lot of the bakery. After unlocking the door and checking that everything was as it should be, he walked Katie in and put her bag down on the floor next to her. "Hey, what's in the bag?"

"A change of clothes."

"Okay." Travis leaned in to kiss her goodbye. One kiss wasn't nearly enough, but he knew it would have to do. Reluctantly waving goodbye, he headed back out the door.

——————FOUR——————

At precisely twelve noon, Travis walked in the back door of the bakery, excited to start his adventure with Katie. He waved a hand to Mrs. O'Neal, who was standing with a young lady near the walk-in that he thought for a moment might be Bella, but her slim profile and strawberry blonde hair told him it was not.

"Hi Mrs. O'Neal. Do you know if Katie is

ready to go?"

Mrs. O'Neal smiled and the young woman with her turned, smiled at him, and then blushed. Several seconds passed before his mind acknowledged what he was seeing and he was a bit shocked to find Katie wearing a tee shirt with a pair of jeans and tennis shoes.

A moment later, before Travis could think of what to say, Mr. O'Neal walked out of the office and stood behind his wife. "Right on time, are you? And eager to be taking our Katie-girl out on a date?"

Somehow, Travis finally found his words, though he still was not certain what to think about the way Katie was dressed. . . and whether or not it was a good thing. "Yeah, Katie and I have plans. That is, unless she's needed here." Seeing both his boss and Katie's in the kitchen, chatting with her, Travis suddenly felt that perhaps his plans were about to be changed.

"Nee, Travis, The O'Neals were just chatting with me about. . . well, about Gwen working more hours. Mrs. O'Neal is going to ask your *mamm* if Gwen can work full time this summer."

"Now don't you worry about that today, Katie. You go have your date with your young man. And I'll be taking my wife home now." Andrew put his arm around Amelia.

Travis nodded and picked up Katie's bag. Then, after a goodbye to the O'Neals, he took her hand and together they walked out to his car. Tossing her bag into the back seat, he moved so Katie could get into her seat, then he gently closed the car door and walked around to his side.

Once he was settled in his seat, he turned to look at her again. She was still his Katie, but there was something about the clothes that gave her a completely different look. He was grateful they were nothing like the getup his sister had shown up in at that singing, but they gave Katie a much more worldly look. In the jeans and tee shirt, she looked like any other girl, especially with her hair uncovered.

"Is something wrong Travis?" Katie's voice shook him out of his thoughts, and since he was not yet sure how he felt about her being dressed so differently, he answered only with a shake of his head before starting the car and slowly pulling out onto the road.

They were to the edge of town before he spoke again. "I don't mind telling you that all morning I expected something to happen to keep us from going out." He laughed as he said it. "Now maybe I can relax and enjoy the day."

"Silly, we've been out on dates a lot the past few months. What makes this one different?"

"I don't know, but I have this strange feeling that it does." He also could not help but wonder if her clothes were some sort of sign or clue that perhaps his feeling was right.

Katie stopped smiling and really looked closely at him. "Maybe it's not us; maybe it's something at home making you feel anxious. Is everyone *allrecht* at home?"

Her question reminded him of one of the things he had been meaning to discuss with her. "Actually, I think it has to do with what you mentioned yesterday. I tried to talk to Gwen on the way to school yesterday, but she kept turning the conversation around to me and you."

Fighting a sudden and unexpected frustration, he took a deep breath before going on. "Then today, she was acting weird. I cleaned the kitchen this morning at the cafe, so I went home to shower and change clothes."

He pulled off the road and put the car in neutral. "Please, before we get into this. . ." He leaned across the seat and captured her lips, hoping that the contact would help center him, as it so often did.

Katie returned the kiss just as she always did, shy at first, relaxing after only a few seconds.

Travis took the opportunity to deepen the kiss, taking her hands in his and placing them against his chest. He could feel his heart pounding against his ribs.

"This is what you do to me, Katie. When I'm kissing you, I feel like my heart beats only for you." And he kissed her again. It was easy to forget where they were, until Katie pushed him away.

Her face was flushed, a soft shade of pink staining her cheeks. "Travis. . . a buggy. I hear a buggy."

Travis noticed a buggy coming towards them from the other direction. He knew it wouldn't look good for Katie if it got back to her family that she was caught kissing on the side of the road. Quickly he put the car in gear and drove off.

"See Katie. No matter where we are, no matter where we go, there's always someone—or something—to interrupt us."

"*Jah,* but maybe *Gott* is sending them to keep us from forgetting ourselves. I hear about *maedels* in the church who get in a family way and have to marry quickly. . ." Katie spoke up. "And we cannot forget Bella and the condition she's in."

Travis nodded his head, but he wasn't completely happy that she made good sense.

Although Travis had taken her hand and was holding it, he didn't say anything else, but he kept glancing over at her. Katie worried that she had said the wrong thing or perhaps should not have dressed like an *Englischer*, but the truth was, she was trying to be with him in his world, while she lived in her world when she wasn't with him.

It was confusing. It was complicated.

When he finally spoke, she heard distress in his voice. "Katie."

"Jah? Was iss letz?"

"Katie, I'm sorry. Please forgive me. You are right. Too often I lose my head when I'm kissing you. Although I try to do the right thing, it's difficult to remember to stop. . . when all I want to do is keep going. I wish. . ." He shook his head and then went on. "But you're right about Bella and the other girls. Things happen sometimes. I don't want that for you."

"It is not just you; I forget everything when you kiss me. If I had not heard the buggy wheels —" She said the words quietly, shame creeping in when she realized it truly was the only thing that had stopped her in that moment.

Travis went on as if he did not notice anything amiss in her voice. "Yes, but it's my responsibility to protect you. I promise you I will try harder. You'll see, I won't forget again tonight. I want you to have a nice memory of our date."

Katie let out a long breath and smiled, even though Travis could likely not see it, since he was looking at the road ahead. "I am having a *gut* time right now. I love taking long drives with you."

"That's part of the plan. The next part is a movie." He smiled over at her when they pulled up at a stop sign. "If I promise to behave like a gentleman, will you go to a movie theater with me?"

"*Jah,* I would like that. Is there something *gut* playing? Are we going to the city?"

He was nodding as he answered. "I checked and there are a couple of movies I think you would enjoy. . . one of them is a Christian film by these two brothers that make movies. I've heard great things about it."

"Wow! That was *wunderbaar!*" Katie wiped at her eyes with a handkerchief. During the movie, Travis had heard her sniffing and had passed her his handkerchief, grateful he had listened when his mom had told him to carry one in his back pocket to use, and one in his shirt pocket to give to Katie in case she needed it.

"Now I thought we would get some supper. Do you like pizza?" Travis hoped she would say yes. After they began dating, they had stayed in town, and as much as he enjoyed living in Abbott Creek, there was not a good pizza place in town.

Travis had been looking forward to introducing Katie to the pizza that had been a big part of his weekly routine when he had lived in the city.

"*Jah,* I've had it several times. I like it a lot."

"Well, it just so happens that I know of a great local pizza place. It's not usually too crowded and they play music, but it's not too loud. So, you can talk, but you don't hear the people around you. Would you like to try it? I think you would enjoy it."

"*Jah,* it sounds *wunderbaar.*"

The pizza place was just as nice as he had described it. The lights were low, with soft music playing in the background, and delicious smells coming from the kitchen area. Once seated, they took a few minutes to look over their menus.

It didn't take long to decide on a large pizza with sausage and mushrooms. The server took their order, then returned with salad and breadsticks, along with their drinks. Travis took Katie's hand and quietly said a prayer before they began eating.

After taking a few bites of his salad, Travis looked up at Katie. "Before I get distracted, maybe we should go ahead and talk about Gwen. I meant to tell you earlier, before we started kissing."

He wiggled his eyebrows and grinned before continuing. "Anyway, I tried to find out if she had a problem at school, or if someone was bothering her, but when I asked her, she said no, that everything was fine. Then she told me to stay out of it and to leave her alone." Travis did not look happy about any of it and Katie tried to find something to say. Her *schweschders* were much too young to have been through any of the things Gwen seemed to be right in the middle of.

Before she could think of anything to say, Travis went on. "Then I decided it might be better to not say anything else, but keep an eye out for anything unusual. And that's when I noticed that she's been on the phone a lot. She takes the phone in her room. . ."

He shrugged as he added, "I guess for privacy, and whenever it rings, she picks it up right away. Whoever it is that's calling her, they must have a lot to say. I was paying attention and the last call was over an hour. . . and for the most part, she talked so low I couldn't really make out anything she said. At least she didn't sound upset; actually, she sounded happy. . . maybe even excited."

"Do you have any idea who she was talking to?" Katie asked, hopeful. Excited was *gut*. Perhaps they had been worrying over nothing.

"Nope. No clue, except she was humming when she came out of her room, until she saw me nearby. Then she grabbed a snack and ran back into her room and closed her door before I could say anything to her. Is this normal for girls?"

"I don't know if I can answer that. I have two young *schweschders*, but we do not share a room and the only phone is in the barn. We typically do not use it much and plain folk tend to keep courting matters to themselves until they are considering marriage. It sounds to me like she is growing up and wants some privacy." She shrugged." Maybe I was worried for no *gut* reason."

"Well, I plan to keep a watch over her. I'd sure like to know who she was talking to on the phone—"

The server arrived with their pizza and they spent the next few minutes eating. Katie really seemed to be enjoying it. Travis felt like he had made good choices today. Who knew when they would have another date like this one, with just the two of them. . .

Once they were back on the road, Travis asked her something that had been on his mind all evening. "Katie, where did you get the English clothes? Did you dress that way for me? Or was there another reason?"

"*Jah,* partly for you. . . and partly for me. I borrowed the jeans from Bella. She can't wear them right now. The tee shirt is one I bought for our date and the shoes I have had for awhile. I have a much plainer pair of tennis shoes that I work in. You've seen them. . ."

Travis nodded and she went on, looking a bit uncomfortable talking about it. "There are really three reasons. . . I wanted you to see what I would look like dressed as an *Englischer*. Plus I wanted to see how I would feel wearing *Englischer* clothes, especially while out around other people. Finally, I didn't want to attract attention on our date the way I do wearing my plain clothes."

"So, part of it was a test, to see if you would you be comfortable wearing jeans and other English clothes?" When she nodded, he went on. "I guess I just never thought about it. For some reason, I just thought you'd always dress the same, but I suppose that's silly."

She looked unsure of herself, as if she had made a mistake. "Well, I—"

Quickly he added, "I have to say, I really like the jeans." Travis felt his cheeks grow hot as thoughts of seeing Katie in tight jeans and slim tee shirts all the time filled his head.

"I like them, too. It's easier to blend in with other people. I like not attracting attention.

That's something that has always bothered me. I'm thinking jeans might be warmer in the winter, too. But I really don't see myself wearing jeans all the time. *Englischers* wear dresses, too." She gave him a searching look. "Which do you prefer to see me wearing?"

"Katie, anything you want to wear is fine with me. I love seeing you in your dresses. But you look really cute in those jeans." Travis hesitated for a moment. "I think it's important for you to choose for yourself; not for me, or your family, or anyone else, but for you."

He gently squeezed her hand. "I just want you to be happy."

———FIVE———

Sunday, after the church service, Katie was busy in the kitchen, helping the others get the kitchen back to the way it was before they served lunch, when Freida came in. Seeing Katie washing dishes at the sink, she hurried over to her.

"I'm glad you came with your family today. . ." Freida pulled Katie away from the dishes, her hands dripping water all across the floor. "So, tell me all about your date with

Travis."

Katie could see that Freida was trying hard not to let the others hear her, which wasn't easy for Freida. "Where did he take you? What all did you do? Did anyone else go with you? What time did you get home?"

"Shh, Freida. Not here." Katie looked around to see who else was nearby who might be able to hear their conversation, much less take notice of her dripping hands. "I cannot talk about it now. Come by the bakery tomorrow and I will answer your questions." As she said it, she made her way back to the sink.

"Tomorrow? I can't wait until tomorrow!"

"You are going to have to, because I am not going to talk about it now. And if you come by the bakery, you can get some peach cobbler. . ."

"*Allrecht*. You know I cannot resist peach cobbler nowadays."

"For now, you can help me finish the dishes

and tell me how you are feeling today. I couldn't help but notice that you went out several times during the service." Katie was worried about her *freind*.

"*Ach.* I'm told that's a normal thing. The bigger the *bopli* gets, the more pressure I feel, which makes me stay close to the bathroom. Thankfully the Zooks have an indoor bathroom now."

Katie giggled with her *freind.* "*Jah.* I can remember a few months ago, you were not so glad when we had services at the Beilers."

"*Ach.* Do not remind me." She put a hand on the bump over her stomach. "I am glad the morning sickness is over."

Katie giggled again. "*Jah.* That was the only time you didn't crave peach cobbler. I'd rather make you cobbler every day than see you feeling so sick every day."

"*Jah.* Now comes the best part. . . . feeling

better again, making clothes and diapers, and getting everything ready."

"*Mamm* has been making diapers for the *boplin*. And not just diapers. I think she's making lots of clothes, especially for Bella's *bopli*. She thinks Bella won't be prepared."

Freida giggled as Katie went on. "*Mamm* has had six children so she knows how many diapers a new *bopli* needs, plus all the clothes and blankets and things."

"*Jah*, my *mamm* is making a quilt for my *bopli*. And I heard her talking to Mary Zook about Bella. The ladies are making a quilt for Bella. Won't she be surprised!" Freida paused a moment before continuing. "And they are planning to take meals over to Mrs. Mueller's house to help out once the *bopli* comes."

"That is a *wunderbaar* idea. Of course everyone will be bringing meals to your house once your *bopli* gets here, too. Is your *mamm* going to stay with you for awhile? Or will she be able to leave your *dat?*"

"*Jah,* she is already planning on it." Freida sighed. "I have been hearing how difficult it can be the first few days, so I am looking forward to having her there to help me." Freida looked anxious. "*Dat* is doing much better now. *Mamm* feared that his cough meant he would have pneumonia again, but the doctor said the cough was just taking longer than usual to go away."

"*Mamm* and I were talking last night about how *wunderbaar* our community is to help anyone in need. When people heard about the trouble the Davis family was having, everyone pitched in and helped, finding jobs for Travis and taking Sissy to the doctor." Katie smiled, thinking of her boyfriend and his family. She quickly continued before Freida could ask about Travis—or their date—again.

"When Bella made her announcement, I

feared that people would judge her, but instead they have taken Bella in and made her and her *bopli* a part of the community."

"Especially Mrs. Mueller." Freida spoke up. "I would never have thought that she would take in a stranger."

Katie was nodding as she added, "Who would have ever guessed that she would take to Bella the way she did. . . and even more surprising, she has stopped gossiping."

Freida jumped in then. *"Jah*. At first, I thought it was just Bella that she wasn't talking about, but I don't think she gossips about anything now."

"That is probably a *gut* thing. We know how gossip can hurt. . . although we never had to worry about not knowing what was going on in the community."

Freida giggled. *"Jah,* that's true, but even so I am glad she has stopped. And the community has been so *gut* about Bella and her condition. Everyone has accepted her, instead of treating her badly. . . just because she made a mistake."

"*Boplin* are to be loved, no matter how they come to us. And we know nothing of Bella or her life before she moved here. Perhaps *Englischers* don't feel that marriage comes before *boplin*. . ." Katie shrugged before adding, "besides, we have had a few *early boplin* in our own community, too."

Anna Miller spoke up from beside them suddenly. Katie and Freida turned to look at their *friend,* surprised at the tone of her voice. "But don't you think it's strange? No one knows anything about her or her family. *Mamm* was surprised when Mrs. O'Neal hired her to work with you at the bakery." She put down the dishes she was packing in a box and turned to them. "Why does she hide her past? Does she have more to hide than just a *bopli?* And where is the father of this *bopli?*"

Katie shook her head, her tone firm. "I have not asked her, and will not. It is her decision to share whatever information she chooses to share."

Anna looked miffed at Katie's answer. "Everyone in the community is talking about her, Katie Chupp. I heard my parents talking about it, too. They are very surprised that your parents allow you to continue working at that bakery." She flounced past them, heading toward the back door, turning back before going outside. "But then, look at what has happened to you. Now you are dating an *Englischer*. . . all because your parents did not take you away from the path of sin, but allowed you to fraternize with the sinner."

"Anna Miller! We are all sinners! There is none greater than another. And Katie has done nothing wrong. She is in her *rumschpringe*. Who are you to judge her or her new *freind*?"

"*Nee,* Freida. My parents thanked *Gott* that you left the bakery and married a *gut* Amish man. But you should have fixed up Katie with one of our *buwes* when you had the chance. I know of several *buwes* that are interested in her, or at least they were before she started dating the *Englischer*." Anna's voice was getting louder as she spoke "Perhaps they will not be so quick to want to court her now."

The bishop's *frau* walked into the kitchen. "*Was iss letz?* We can hear you outside. That is no way to act on the Lord's day."

Katie was quick to respond. "We're sorry, Mary. We should have been more careful."

"*Nee,* I was telling Katie and Freida how the community feels about Bella. Katie should quit her job, join the church and find a *gut* Amish man to court. . . and marry. *Mamm* and *Dat* said —"

"Anna, you should not be repeating things that you hear your *mamm* and *dat* talk about. And Katie should be certain of what she wants before she joins the church. I am thinking this is why she is dating the *Englischer,* because she is not yet certain that it is the thing to do." When she went on, her voice was softer, and her expression held more understanding than Katie would ever have expected from any of their leadership. "We must all follow our hearts, *jah?*"

Katie could only nod. Anna's words had hurt, but she was not surprised by them, especially after what had already been said about her decorations on the bakery window. However, it was more than a little surprising to hear what sounded like encouragement for her to date Travis. . . from Mary. . . the Bishop's *frau.* But her words made sense, and it was what the preachers said in church. . . to be certain before taking a step that is, for all accounts, an irreversible commitment.

Anna huffed out a breath and pushed through the kitchen door, allowing it to smack shut behind her. Mary walked over and put an arm around Katie's shoulders. "Just you remember, Katie Chupp, it is much better to choose the *Englisch* world now, before you are baptized, than to dedicate yourself to our ways and then change your mind."

When Katie looked up at her, Mary smiled and then continued. "We want you to be a part of the community. . . ." Then, she leaned closer and added, "whether it be plain or *Englisch.*"

With one final squeeze, she let go and followed Anna.

Katie and Freida stood for several minutes, just looking after her. Then they looked at each other and burst into a fit of giggles.

But Katie realized, now more than ever, that she had some serious thinking ahead of her.

Later that evening, after Katie and her family had finished supper, her *dat* approached her.

"Katie, your *mamm* and I would like to speak with you. Maybe we should go back to the kitchen while the others are outside doing their chores."

Katie followed her parents into the kitchen. After sitting back down at the table that had recently held their supper, Caleb looked over at his *frau* before turning back to Katie.

"*Dochder,* there is much talk among the plain people concerning the situation in town. . . and our family. The bishop sought me out to ask if you are going to join the next class in order to be baptized." When Katie opened her mouth to speak, he put his hand up to stop her. After a few seconds, he continued.

"He also said that some of the men have spoken to him about the new counter person at the bakery and her condition. They shared their concerns about your working so closely with her, especially since you are now the only plain employee at the bakery. Indeed, you are now working only with this young *maedel,* along with the *buwe* you are dating, his *schweschder,* and your employer."

Martha got up from the table and began to prepare *kaffe.* She glanced over at Katie, gave her a timid smile, then turned away.

Caleb's voice was quiet, yet firm when he added, "Katie, we feel it is best at this time for you to give your notice at the bakery so Amelia can replace you with someone more. . . suitable."

Katie looked at her *dat,* more than a bit

stunned. Katie knew that Mrs. O'Neal depended on her. She did all of the baking. What would Mrs. O'Neal do if she left?

The bakery would likely close. Many of the plain folks could bake as well as Katie or better, but no one she knew would be willing to dedicate so much of their time to baking, especially when it would not be for their own family.

She tried to say that very thing to her *dat,* and still be respectful of him. "But *Dat,* Mrs. O'Neal would never have opened the bakery if not for Freida and me. She said she wanted to offer the baked goods and desserts to the whole town that Freida and I sold at her parents' roadside stand."

"That makes no difference now. Things have changed, as you know. Things are very different there. Not too long ago, you and Freida worked together, without anyone else around, except for

Amelia Simpkins. When she hired Travis, your *mamm* and I talked about you leaving the bakery. . . then when you painted the pictures on the window at Christmas—"

"Caleb, are you sure we need to do this?"

"*Jah*, Martha. I am sure. I just wish we had done this before Katie got the notion to date the *Englischer*. Then maybe she would have already joined the church and be married to Marvin or David Schmidt, or perhaps one of the Yoder *buwes*, or one of the other *buwes* in the community."

Katie felt panic take hold of her. They were not just wanting her to give up her job then. They were wanting her to give up Travis as well.

She struggled to control the tears that were suddenly filling her eyes. "*Dat*, I was never interested in one of the Schmidt *buwes* or the Yoder *buwes*, or any of the other *buwes* in the community. Travis Davis is the only *buwe* to catch my attention. I did not try to seek the attention of him, or any other *Englisch buwe,* but he is the only *buwe* I am interested in courting. I don't know what the future holds for us, but I know he is important to me."

"But *dochder,* he is an *Englischer!*" Martha spoke quietly, without accusation, but her voice held a sadness that Katie could hardly bear.

"*Jah,* he is an *Englischer.* And I did not plan to court an *Englischer,* but I cannot help it that he is one." Katie took a deep breath before continuing. "But *Mamm,* even if he wasn't, I do not know if I will ever take my vows and be baptized. The bishop told me that I must be certain—and I am not."

"*Nee,* you were fine until you started hanging out with that *buwe.* . . he has turned your thoughts from the plain world to the *Englisch* world." The sound of shame in her *dat's* voice was near to breaking Katie's heart.

This was the one thing she had not looked forward to, the one worry she had never shared with Travis, the thing that could bring all of his worries to bear, having to choose between her family and the man she loved.

"*Dat,* you don't understand. It's not that the *Englisch* world is tempting me. . . not really. And it's not Travis. If he were plain, I would still not be ready."

Caleb jumped to his feet, knocking over his chair. Smacking his closed fists on the table, he shouted, "I don't believe that! I cannot accept that!"

"I am sorry, *Dat.* I must choose. . . and I have chosen the *Englisch* world." The words tumbled out, and though they surprised her, Katie realized they were completely the truth. This was what she had been preparing for. She had just not been ready to admit it to herself.

Quickly, she walked out, practically running

up the stairs to her bedroom. Before closing her door, she heard her *mamm* speaking.

"Let her go, Caleb. We cannot force her to choose our way. We can only pray for her, that *Gott* will guide her, that she will make the right decision."

When she heard a door slam, Katie gently closed her door and moved towards her bed, falling to her knees.

Dear Gott, please help Mamm and Dat, and my family, to understand that I'm not trying to hurt them or be disrespectful. But I cannot make the commitment to the church that they are asking me—expecting me—to make.

I do not want to lose my family, or my freinden, but I feel like I am making the right choice in not taking my vows, but going down another path. Please give me the courage to do what I feel led to do. . .

—————— SIX ——————

Monday morning, after dropping Amelia off at the bakery and chatting with Katie and Bella for a few minutes, Andrew headed across the street to the Irish Blessings Cafe.

Looking around downstairs and not finding Sean, he headed upstairs to the office. When he walked in, Sean was hurriedly putting his wallet away, and he had a strange look on his face.

"Morning, nephew." With a laugh, he added,

"I expected to find you downstairs, perhaps in the kitchen, having your third cup of coffee."

"Now don't ya be makin fun of me because I'm not a morning person. I canna help it if I need coffee before I can wake up and face the world. . . or at least. . . customers." Sean had barely gotten the words out before a huge yawn stopped further comments.

"I have news for ya, Sean. Even after you've had several cups of coffee, you're still not a morning person. But since you're running the cafe just fine, I have no complaints."

Sean's face fairly lit up before he cleared his throat and turned away, pretending to pat himself on the back. "Thanks. I'll take that compliment, since I know how hard I've been workin to do a good job for ya."

Andrew laughed at his nephew's antics and said nothing about his obvious excitement at Andrew's praise. "All right now. Let's head down to the kitchen for some of that delicious coffee, why don't we. I've got a few things to do here before I head out to run errands."

Sean nodded and moved to the stairs, stepping ahead when Andrew motioned for him. "Be sure to watch out for extra traffic, Uncle; today is the last day of school and you'll be running errands about the same time that school lets out."

"I don't plan to be running errands that late. I should be done by a bit after lunchtime."

"Yeah, that's why I warned ya, because school is only half a day today." Sean insisted, picking up his mug from the shelf over the sink and moving to the counter to pour coffee.

"How do you know so much about school and when it lets out, or when the last day comes?" Andrew puzzled over it while pouring his own coffee. "Who do you know who still attends school?" It was more than a little curious that

Sean knew anything about the local schools.

"Uh, Travis must have mentioned something about his sister—his brothers and sister—getting out early today because it's the last day of school." Sean answered, but did not meet Andrew's searching look.

Andrew also thought it strange that Sean's face looked suddenly flushed. . . but told himself perhaps it was the hot coffee his nephew had quickly downed.

"Speaking of the Davis family. . ." Andrew left the words hanging there, hoping to elicit a response from his elusive nephew.

"Aye?" Was the only response Sean made though. "Well, that's one of my errands today. It's been too long since we dropped in on them, don't ya think?"

Sean said nothing so Andrew went on. "And it's one reason I dropped by to talk to you. You always enjoy visiting the Davis family as much as I do. . . would you be wanting to go with me?"

"Sure, I could find time for it, I think." Sean's response stirred Andrew's curiosity again. He had always enjoyed visiting with the Davis family. What could be going on that had him sounding like it would be a chore?

"All right then. Let's go on over and visit with Mrs. Davis. I'd like to know how she's doing." Andrew moved toward the door, then looked back at his nephew, who hadn't moved.

"Actually, I was hoping to get a few things done here before we go. If it's okay with you, let's wait until after the lunch crowd is over and then go."

Andrew blew out a breath. "I thought you said I should try to be done with everything before lunch because of the school letting out early. Why should we wait? I'd really rather go on now and get it done."

"Well then, in that case, you go on ahead. I'll beg off today and go with ya another time." Sean turned to the sink, rinsing out his coffee mug. . . even though it had not been completely empty.

"Sean, I know you're not exactly a morning person, but you might consider another cup of coffee. You're not makin much sense this mornin."

When Sean said nothing, Andrew pressed. "I was really hoping you'd go with me. I expected you to go. . . you're usually eager to visit them. What's going on with you today?"

"Nothing.   Nothing."   Sean   looked uncomfortable. He poured himself another cup of coffee before turning back towards his uncle. "Uncle, we have never went this early before. Isn't it just possible Mrs. Davis isn't ready for company this soon? Not everyone is an early riser like you."

Andrew stood there, not sure what to say.

Surely it wasn't that early. What was going on with his nephew?

However, after nearly a minute of just standing in the kitchen, staring at his nephew, finally he gave in. "Well, all right. I'll go run my other errands this morning and come by to pick you up around one o'clock. Then we'll run over to visit the Davis clan. Does that work better for you?"

"Sure, that works fine. I'll be ready at one."

After his uncle had left, Sean noticed the cup of cold coffee from earlier and reached to pour it out. When he picked up the mug, he noticed his hand shaking a bit.

Whew! This is really getting to me! It was hard enough trying to run a cafe with hardly any experience. *Although it seems to be going great. .*

.

But with trying to make this thing work. . . *while hiding it from everyone.* It was enough to drive a man crazy! *Almost enough even to make a man swear off women. . . except then there'd be nothing to look forward to each day!*

And his uncle had almost caught him looking at the pictures in his wallet. *What would he think of me if he knew. . . he surely wouldn't understand.*

Sooner or later, it would all come out and everyone would have a fit. *I don't think anyone will approve of it. But what else can I do? I'll just have to hide it for as long as I can. . . then I guess I'll have to face the consequences.* He rubbed a hand over his face. *Oh man, what a mess!*

I wish I could tell Uncle Andrew; he might understand, considering he got involved with someone a lot older than he was, and then he married her. But without being sure he would be on their side, it was not a risk Sean could take. *He might fire me and send me straight back home!*

Sean knew age differences could be a big deal; which was precisely why they were trying to hide their relationship. *Not that we have much of one now. . . he* thought bitterly.

Someday, when the time is right. . . when our families might be more understanding. . . we could. . . maybe.

There was something about her that made him feel strong and brave. . . and more like a man than he'd ever felt before. . . but he didn't want to do anything to get her into any trouble.

She cared for him; he knew she did. She had given him several pictures; he also had ones he had taken with his own camera. He still remembered the thrill when she had asked him to print two copies of some of the pictures, so that she could have copies of the ones they were both in. . . and the few she had taken of him as well.

He had barely breathed that afternoon, listening over the whir of the printer in the office, praying his uncle wouldn't come up to check on him while he waited for the slow contraption to finish the job.

He had been bold enough to ask if he could take a picture of her. Then she had talked him into letting her take one of him—for her diary, she had said. And she had asked if he knew how to do selfies. . . when he said he did, she asked him to take one of them together.

He loved the way they looked together.

——SEVEN——

When Mrs. Mueller arrived at the bakery the next morning, Katie just happened to be out front. Bella would be leaving for her weekly checkup soon and Ada always accompanied her.

Katie watched as Mrs. O'Neal chatted with Mrs. Mueller and Bella, marveling in the change that Bella's arrival had caused in the woman. Keeping secrets wasn't something Ada Mueller had been known for. As long as Katie or anyone else in town she could think of could remember, she was the one person in town who could be counted on to spread gossip, whether the individual wanted the news to be shared or not.

However, since Bella Stanton had shown up on her doorstep almost seven months ago, Mrs. Mueller had been keeping lots of secrets.

Katie knew that Mrs. O'Neal had been more than a little worried about Bella continuing to work at the bakery. She had spoken first to Bella, then to Katie, and finally to Freida about it, but wasn't satisfied with the responses she received.

She had even gone so far as to call the doctor's office, but they had informed her that they weren't allowed to share any information with her about her employee or her condition; nor would they give her any basic advice concerning the subject. Finally she'd gone to Mrs. Mueller, who had suggested she go along with them to the next appointment, if Bella agreed.

After her husband dropped her off at the bakery, Mrs. O'Neal had shared the news with Katie that she would be leaving at nine-thirty with Bella and Mrs. Mueller.

"Gwen is here to help you and Freida told me she'd come in at ten o'clock today, so you should have plenty of help for now. We should be back by lunchtime, according to Bella."

"Freida is coming today? That is *gut*." Katie was relieved to hear it. There was much to do in the kitchen. "I think I will ask Gwen to wait on the customers until Bella returns. She has had lots of practice out front and should be able to handle the customers with no problems. I can use Freida's help with the baking today."

Katie enjoyed working with Freida and she needed to talk to her *friend* without anyone close by who would hear their conversation. This would be the perfect chance to share what had been going on recently.

"And we both know this will give Freida a chance to fill up on more peach cobbler," laughed Amelia. "My word, I don't think I ever took stock in pregnancy cravings until recently."

Katie nodded, laughing along with her boss.

"But Freida and Bella have made a believer out of me with their constant cravings."

"It's a *gut* thing our customers have not ordered peach cobbler very often. More often than not, Freida and Bella don't leave much for anyone else." Katie laughed again, but there was no response from Amelia.

Katie followed the direction of her gaze and saw that she was looking over to where Bella stood with Mrs. Mueller and Gwen, all three of them laughing over something.

Bella had a hand pressed against her large belly and, somehow, Katie was certain that was where her boss's eyes were trained. Concerned, Katie spoke up, her voice quiet so that only Mrs.

O'Neal would hear. "Is everything *allrecht,* Mrs. O'Neal?"

It was a moment before Amelia looked back to where Katie stood, the wet cloth she had been using to wipe down the counters hanging limply from one hand. "Yes, dear girl, everything is fine. Sometimes my thoughts travel back to the past without any warning."

Katie watched as her boss turned to watch Bella again. She did not really expect Amelia to speak again, but she did and her words were very quiet. . . almost too quiet for Katie to hear.

"You see, although we wanted them, my Henry and I could never have children." Katie could see her boss's eyes bright with unshed tears. "And Henry didn't want to adopt. It was a disappointment to me, but—" She shrugged, but Katie could hear the sadness in her voice.

Before Katie could say a word, Amelia hurried off to her office, returning after only a minute with one of her lace handkerchiefs. "I'm sorry, Katie. With both Freida and Bella expecting, I suppose babies have been on my mind lately. And now. . . well, with Andrew. . . his wife passed before they could have children." She shrugged again, wiping away tears as she did so. "And I am much too old to have a child now, even if it were possible."

A long, heavy moment passed before Amelia cleared her throat and pasted on a bright smile. "Anyway, now I have you girls." She turned and put an arm around Katie's shoulders, squeezing gently. "You are all like family to me—and to Andrew. He thinks the world of you girls. Plus we have Sean now. . . plus Travis and his brothers and sisters. Why, our family is actually quite large, when you think about it!"

When Amelia laughed, Katie joined her. For nearly a minute, they laughed together and this time, when Amelia spoke, she sounded much happier. "Well, Katie, I will let you get back to work now. You have a peach cobbler to make, I believe. And I had better not keep Bella and Ada waiting. We would not want her to be late for the doctor."

"*Jah.*" Katie watched Amelia straighten her shoulders and march over to where the trio stood, still talking and laughing. There was so much going on with her sweet boss that she would never have guessed at. *Clearly Mrs. O'Neal has been through much more than I ever knew. No wonder she is such a strong woman.*

Katie said something about getting the cobbler done before Freida arrived, but Mrs. O'Neal was already standing by the talking, laughing trio of women by then.

A minute later, after the front door had closed behind them and Gwen had moved behind the counter, Katie pushed through the swinging doors into the kitchen and dove back into her baking.

Amelia wasn't sure what to expect when she accompanied Bella to her weekly appointment, but everything quickly fell into place. She and Ada waited outside while Bella went back for the routine checkup, then they were called into the doctor's office for a few minutes.

"I understand you have a few questions," the kind-looking, older doctor quietly stated.

"Yes. Bella works in my bakery," began Amelia, looking to Bella to be certain she was all right with her boss asking questions of such a personal nature. Bella nodded and Amelia went on "I'm mostly concerned with how long she should continue working. I expected by now she would be taking maternity leave."

The doctor smiled and answered. "I understand perfectly. What you have to understand is, as long as her work isn't too strenuous and she doesn't have to lift anything heavy, Bella can continue to work as long as she is comfortable doing her job. Right up until her due date is fine, as long as she is comfortable with it, or more precisely, until she goes into labor. As long as this is all right with you. . . and she chooses to do so."

"I see. Well, we are all trying to make certain she is taking rest breaks, and she is not allowed to pick up or carry anything heavy. I certainly have no problem with her continuing to work as long as she chooses to, and and I'm certain the other employees feel the same. I just wanted to be sure, as her employer, that it was all right to allow her to continue working."

The doctor smiled then, and went on. "I appreciate your concern. Honestly, I wish more employers had their employee's best interest in mind. Too often, I see young women who—well, never mind." He waved a hand in the air before going on. "I am glad to see that Bella has such an employer who is considerate of her, especially after everything she has been through."

Before Amelia could say anything, Ada stood up. "Amelia, if you're satisfied with the doctor's assurance that Bella can continue to work, I think it's time we let him get back to his other patients."

"Yes, of course. Thank you, Doctor." Amelia stood up and followed Ada and Bella into the hallway.

"I know you may have other questions, but perhaps this isn't the time and place for them."

Amelia could see by the expression on Ada's face that she was hoping Amelia would not press further. Turning to Bella, she only said, "All right. Bella dear, are you ready to leave? Or is there anything else you need to do while you're here?"

Oddly, Bella looked anything but happy at the moment. "I'm done here. . . ready to get back to work."

"Perhaps we should stop for a bite of lunch before taking you back to work, dear. You must keep up your strength."

Bella's only response was a terse nod. And, when Amelia looked to Ada, she shook her head slowly back and forth, which was clearly her way of telling Amelia now was not a good time to press Bella.

Amelia was not ready to give up so easily. And while she didn't want to upset Bella, she had hoped that when Ada had invited her to join them, it would be so that she would find more answers.

"I suppose we could just go back to the Sweet Shop. I am only thinking of your health and well-being, Bella." She pushed through the main door of the doctor's office, Ada and Bella right behind her.

When they reached Bella's car, Amelia turned to look at the two of them. Ada stood there looking at Amelia, and Amelia looked right back at her.

After a minute, Ada turned to Bella, putting an arm around the young woman. "Bella, I think it's time you confided a little in Amelia. She won't speak of anything you say, not even to Andrew or your friends at work. . . unless you ask her to." She looked back to Amelia, who nodded her agreement.

"I know, but it's just so embarrassing to talk about. Would you. . . could you. . . help me?" Bella's cheeks were flushed and Amelia was suddenly concerned. Whatever it was Ada wanted her to confide in Amelia about was certainly not more important than her health.

"Bella, if you'd rather not talk about it, I will understand. I don't want you to feel that you have to tell me anything you don't want me to know."

"No, Miss Ada is right. It's time to tell you." Bella gave a little shaky laugh. "It's probably way past time to talk to you. I just kept putting it off. But I'd rather talk about it now and get it over and done."

"All right, dear. Why don't we go back to my house. I'll have Andrew fix us up a nice, light lunch from Irish Blessings, then after he leaves, we can have our talk."

"That sounds nice, doesn't it, Bella?" Ada smiled at Bella, then winked at Amelia as Bella nodded slowly, saying nothing.

"Let me just call him now and we can eat as soon as we arrive." Amelia took out her phone and a moment later, Andrew answered. "Andrew dear, would you be so kind as to make up a lunch for Ada, Bella and me. We're going to have lunch at our house before we take Bella back to work."

To his credit, if Andrew noticed anything odd in her voice, he did not mention it. He only asked if everyone would like their usual and told Amelia he would be right along, and in less than a minute, she said goodbye and put the phone back into her purse.

"He is going to drop off the food in a bit. He may even beat us home." She laughed as she said it, thankful once again to live so close to town.

By then, they were all in the car, so Ada pulled out of the parking lot and turned toward home.

<h1 style="text-align:center">——— EIGHT ———</h1>

Katie was surprised when Mrs. O'Neal called to say that Bella wouldn't be coming back to work. Bella always came back to work after her doctor appointments. . .

Until now anyway.

"I hope everything is *allrecht*. Will she be back tomorrow or did the doctor say that she needs to stop working now?" Katie tried to keep her questions simple, though she secretly hoped that her boss had been able to get some information out of Mrs. Mueller, Bella's doctor or Bella herself about what was really going on with the young woman.

Amelia was quick to assure her that everything was fine. "Bella's appointment went well. And yes, she will be back to work tomorrow. We stopped for lunch, and afterward Bella looked a little tired, so I sent her home to rest. I won't be back today, either." Mrs. O'Neal suddenly sounded very tired, so much so that Katie began to worry about her boss's health as well. "I'll see you tomorrow, dear."

Whatever happened today?

Katie wondered, but she didn't dare ask. She only said goodbye and hung up the phone, looking over at Freida, who was sitting at the counter with a concerned expression of her own. "Mrs. O'Neal says Bella looked tired after they had lunch, so she sent her home to rest. She won't be back today."

"Well, that makes sense." Freida nodded as she answered, and Katie walked over to the sink to wash her hands. "I get tired a lot more often now, and Bella's baby is almost due. She must get tired even more often than I do." A moment later she added, "I am really surprised that she is still working. When is she going to quit? Did she say?"

"I don't know. She hasn't said anything to me about quitting." Katie went back to mixing the cookie dough she had been working on when the phone rang. "I thought Mrs. O'Neal was going to ask the doctor today how much longer Bella can work. . . at least, that was the idea I got from what she said. I guess perhaps we'll find out tomorrow."

"I suppose." Freida seemed oddly satisfied with the answer, which left Katie wondering if she was perhaps a bit overly concerned about

Bella and her situation.

While she stirred the thick dough, and Freida ate her peach cobbler, Katie thought about babies. . . and Bella. . . and about what Anna and her parents had spoken to her about on Sunday. Freida had been right there with her when Anna had spoken so harshly, though she likely had not heard what Mary had told her only moments later. And Katie had not been able to bring herself to share her parents' words with her *freind*. There was still so much about that conversation that hurt.

Resisting the urge to rub a hand over her face at the sudden frustration she felt, Katie could not help but think of how absurd it all was. She had enjoyed a *wunderbaar* evening with Travis on Saturday and then, on *Gott's* day of all things, her parents had essentially told her they expected her to stop seeing him and quit her job.

What would Mrs. O'Neal do without me here?

She wanted to think that her sweet boss could find someone in the community who could replace her, but the thought of not coming to work at the bakery week after week nearly broke Katie's heart.

She could not even bear to think about the idea of never seeing Travis again.

Since Mrs. O'Neal had left with Bella and Ada, Gwen had spent most of her time out front waiting on customers while Katie and Freida had spent most of their time in the kitchen, talking about Katie's date on Saturday.

Katie didn't mind Gwen hearing about it, but thinking of the possibility that she would have to stop seeing Travis soon, she was afraid to let his sister get too attached to the idea of Katie and Travis becoming a more serious couple.

Heaven knows she has had enough sadness and strife in her young life already.

It took Katie completely by surprise, when

Gwen stepped across the street to pick up lunch for the three girls, and Freida brought up the subject of Anna Miller.

It did not take long for Katie to realize that now was the time to tell her *freind* about the talk she'd had with her parents on Sunday evening.

"Wow!" Freida sat, staring at Katie for nearly a minute before going on. "What are you going to do?"

"Nothing." Katie shook her head, only just now realizing that the answer had always been there. "I cannot join the church right now, no matter how much *Mamm* and *Dat*. . . or others . . . might want me to."

"So. . ." Freida was nodding, but her face was full of uncertainty. "What happens now? Will you stay in the community? Will you have to leave home?"

"I don't know. I have put most of the money

I made at work in a savings account at the bank, saving for when I get married."

Freida nodded and Katie went on. "*Mamm* and *Dat* always encouraged me to save money, and there are several people in town who rent small apartments or rooms, so I should be able to support myself well enough if I need to."

"*Jah,* and Mrs. Mueller sometimes has rooms to rent, doesn't she? Bella is only in one of them." Freida sounded excited for a moment, but by the time she had finished speaking, the excitement had drained away, leaving sadness behind.

"All of it sounds *verrickt* to me. I don't want to live alone; I want to be with my family." Katie could hardly believe she was even thinking about these things. Only two days ago, everything had felt absolutely perfect in her life. Now she was considering moving away from home and being all on her own. "I am beginning to realize why

Bella seems sad so often."

"*Jah.*" was all Freida said.

They remained silent for several minutes. The only sound was Katie's wire whisk brushing against the edge of the metal mixing bowl.

"All I can think is to pray that *Gott* will help my parents understand how I feel. And that they will allow me to continue living with them."

Freida moved down from her stool and walked around the table to give her *freind* a hug. "I will pray this, too. I feel partly responsible, since I kept at you to date Travis."

"*Nee,* this is not because of Travis." Katie insisted.

"Are you sure, Katie. . . really sure?"

"*Jah,* I am. I enjoy spending time with Travis and I hope to keep on spending time with him, but if I were not involved with him, I would still not be ready to be baptized and join the church." She watched her *freind* carefully as she said the next words.

"Why do you think I was so quick to take this job, Freida? This is not a job I can easily quit. Mrs. O'Neal is counting on me to do the baking. I work six days most weeks. I knew that when I accepted her offer. Most *maedels* would not take such a permanent job just as they are coming to the end of their *rumschpringe*. I did, because I knew I was not ready and I hoped it would give me time to figure some things out."

"What do you mean?" Freida looked puzzled.

"I mean. . . . just what happened with you and your Thomas. You knew what you wanted when you took the job."

"*Jah,* I only took it to save money."

"Right." Katie insisted. "You knew you wanted to be married, and you wanted to save some money. *Mamm* and *Dat* thought the same for me, and I did save the money, but I always sort of thought I might need it to take care of myself when the time came if they decided it would be time for me to move away from home."

"*Jah,* but Katie, surely they will not make you move away just because you have not yet made up your mind."

"That is my prayer."

Again, they both remained quiet for what felt like a long time before Freida spoke again. "Please just do not take your vows and then leave. I can handle it if you decide not to join the church, but I could not take it if the church were to shun you." She took hold of Katie's hands, pulling the whisk out of her grip when she did. "I need my best freind."

Katie hugged Freida then. "I do, too. I don't want to think what I would do without your friendship. . . without you to talk to."

"Well, as long as you don't take your vows, no one should have a reason to shun you, or treat you any differently."

"We both know it still happens." Katie could not help it—she had to voice the fear, to get it out in the open where she could face it.

"*Jah,* it does. But not in our community, at least so far." Freida looked up as the back door opened. "I think I'll see if there's anything to do out front."

Watching her as she grabbed her bowl of peach cobbler before moving on past the swinging doors, Katie smiled for the first time in awhile.

"She sure loves your cobbler."

Katie gasped at the deep, masculine voice she knew so well by now.

Without giving Katie time to say anything, Travis turned her around. Leaning down, he touched his lips to hers, setting off a spark.

Katie's eyes closed as she relished the sensation of his lips on hers while she eagerly kissed him back. Her arms tightened around his neck as she felt his hands caressing her back.

They jerked apart at the sound of a knock at the door. A moment later, Gwen walked in. "I saw the truck out back, so I thought I'd better knock before entering, just in case." She giggled. "Yep, you both look like you've been kissing."

"Go away, little sister. Go help Freida." As he moved closer to Katie again, they both heard laughter coming from out front. Katie cringed a little. Travis and Gwen might not know Freida well enough by now, but she could tell that the laughter was forced.

Freida is still worrying.

"Come help me, Gwen. Give those two lovebirds a few minutes alone." Her voice held a note of tension too, but Katie was certain the brother and sister would never notice.

Laughing, Gwen ran past her brother. "Fine. But only for a few minutes, big brother, then I'm coming back. Katie and Freida need to eat their lunches."

Travis gathered Katie to him in a gentle hug, resting her head against his shoulder. She leaned close, enjoying the feeling of being so close to him, but also the feeling that she was safe. . . protected. . . loved.

"Now where were we?" Finding her lips again, he proceeded to kiss her until she forgot everything around her, which was a blessed relief.

All too soon though, the sound of the bell over the front door rang and he ended the kiss, pulling her against him once more in a quick hug before letting go and stepping back.

Katie turned back to the bowl of dough just as Freida walked through the swinging doors, a knowing smile on her face.

"The mayor's wife is here to pick up that special cake she ordered. It's in the walk-in, *jah?*" Freida asked. Thankfully, she was looking at Katie, so she saw Katie nod.

A hard knot had formed in Katie's throat along with the tears that had sprang to her eyes, and she was more grateful than ever that Freida knew her so well.

"All right, sweetheart. You sit down a minute. . . and enjoy your lunch." With another quick kiss, Travis gathered the boxes stacked at the back door and left to make his deliveries.

—————NINE—————

After work on Thursday, Travis took Katie to visit his family. At least once a week, Katie enjoyed getting together with the Davis family, usually on Thursdays.

Travis would come by the bakery a little after closing time, giving the girls time to clean up and prep for the next day. Then he would drive Katie, and more often than not his sister, home to spend the rest of the evening with his mother and little brothers.

Seven-year-old Bobby had claimed a special place in Katie's heart when she'd first met him almost two years ago.

After the bakery had been robbed, the last thing she had expected was to see a small child sitting on the front steps of a rundown house, eating a blueberry cupcake that had been stolen from the bakery. A cupcake she recognized because of the unique wrapper that her boss ordered for a special customer.

The Davis family had suffered a great loss with the death of the children's dad six months before. Then their mom had been sick for several months.

Fortunately, when Travis had returned home to care for his family, things had gotten better. It had also helped that the community had followed Amelia and Andrew O'Neal's example and taken the family under their collective wings.

First, Mrs. O'Neal had given him a part-time job at the bakery as their delivery person. Of course, she had been Mrs. Simpkins then. Katie could still remember the odd looks Travis had given Andrew O'Neal when he had come by with sandwiches and other food on his many visits to the family.

Travis was likely not the only Davis who had been thrilled to discover that the cafe owner had been much more interested in the bakery owner than in Mrs. Davis.

Travis had stayed busy doing odd jobs around the community between deliveries and it had not taken long at all for him to get to know quite a few people in the town. He had worked several times for the Yoders. Mr. O'Neal had also hired him part time making deliveries for his cafe, Irish Blessings.

When Mr. O'Neal followed Mrs. Simpkins to New York, his nephew Sean had been forced to take over running the cafe. . . and he had called on Travis for help. Upon his return, Andrew had been impressed with him and had asked him to take on more responsibility at the cafe, so Travis was working full time there now.

His sister Gwen had started working at the bakery part-time just before Thanksgiving and she was doing a great job. The customers liked her and she loved to learn about baking the breads, cookies, cakes, and other treats that the bakery sold.

Katie had thought that everyone was as fond of the Davis family as she was, at least until Anna's comments on Sunday.

Katie was always glad to see the improvements in Cissy Davis. It had taken her such a long time to recover from the loss of her husband, and then her serious bout with pneumonia, but she was doing fine now.

She was waiting at the door when Gwen, Travis and Katie arrived. "Welcome, Katie. It is so good to see you." She folded Katie into a hug, and the strength in her slim arms surprised Katie. "Bobby has been helping me with supper."

"That sounds *wunderbaar!*" Katie gushed. "Where is my little buddy?"

"Here I am, Katie!" shouted Bobby, running down the hall to the door. Once he reached her, he threw his arms around Katie and hugged her like he hadn't seen her in months.

"Bobby, you are getting so big! I think you must have grown another inch since last week." Katie teased him. "My goodness, you'll be taller than me soon."

"Yeah, I will. I'm growing a lot." He made a show of walking on his tip-toes, trying to tower over her and Katie even slouched a little to play along. It was a surprise to see they were nearly the same height that way. *Goodness. He will be as tall as me soon.*

"Well, let's go in and eat supper before it gets cold." Cissy ushered the four of them toward the dining room as she added, "You need to eat good, nourishing food if you plan to grow as tall as your big brothers some day." Gwen gave Bobby a push, laughing when he wouldn't let go of Katie.

"Come on, Katie. You can sit by me." Bobby tugged at her arm, pulling her to the table.

"Bobby, stop yanking on Katie's arm. You know she always sits by you." Travis said with a sigh.

Katie leaned in toward Travis, speaking softly. "It's *allrecht*. Bobby and I have a special relationship." Leaning even closer, she whispered, "I think he might be a bit jealous of you, since we are dating."

She smiled when he winked at her. Quickly she sat down next to Bobby. Travis sat down and leaned towards Katie, putting his arm around her to pat his brother on the back.

"We have her just where we want her now, pard." As Travis leaned back, Katie felt a kiss as light as an angel's wings brush the top of her head.

Cissy had prepared a delicious supper of meatloaf, sliced tomatoes, green peas, and mashed potatoes with cheese and just a touch of garlic. And, since Katie rarely got macaroni and cheese at home, Cissy always added it to the menu when she came for supper.

Katie always insisted on bringing bread and a dessert to add to the meal. Gwen had asked today if they could bring yeast rolls to go with the meatloaf. Along with a couple dozen rolls, Katie and Gwen had chosen chocolate cupcakes for the children and lemon-filled danishes for the adults. Knowing it was Bobby's favorite treat, Katie had also brought along a bag of sugar cookies, which she had hidden in her bag.

"Travis, will you please ask the blessing for the food?" Cissy spoke softly, looking to her eldest son as the man of the family.

Travis bowed his head and begun praying immediately. The first few times he had brought her home for dinner, it had been somewhat of a shock to hear him praying aloud, but Katie was beginning to really enjoy hearing him speak out loud to *Gott* like a flesh-and-blood father. . . . as if He was there in the room with them.

"Lord, we thank you for this food and ask you to bless it. Thank you for supplying our needs and for the many friendships we have here in Abbott Creek. Most of all, I thank you for my family and my Katie-girl. In Jesus' name I pray. Amen." As he spoke, he squeezed Katie's hand

and she felt a little thrill rush through her at their shared connection.

After supper, Katie followed Cissy into the kitchen to help with dishes, but Gwen shooed her back into the dining room, where everyone else had gathered around the table to work on a puzzle.

There was lots of chatter, and though the actual piecing went slowly, the puzzle was finally completed, to the delight of the kids. Katie took the opportunity when everyone scattered, to slip Bobby his small bag of cookies.

He jumped up and Katie worried he might attract the attention of the others, so she put a finger to her lips and reminded him the cookies were their secret.

Fortunately, he took her cue and quieted right down. Though he did throw his arms around Katie and give her a tight hug before carrying the bag off to his room with a grin.

Travis walked back into the room just as Bobby went out. "And just what was that all about?"

Katie smiled and looked down at her feet, while putting the most innocent expression she could muster on her face. "I'm certain I don't know what you are referring to."

"Oh, you are. . . . I think you know exactly what I'm talking about, Katie-girl." He moved forward and slipped his arms around her, nipping playfully at her nose.

The moment his lips touched hers, there was the sound of feet pounding hard on the floor above them, and just before three boys came running into the dining room, Travis let her go and stepped back.

Bobby ran through the room a moment later, his brothers only inches behind him. There were shouts and more pounding feet as Travis grabbed Sam and Trevor, bringing the stampede to a halt. "That is enough of that inside. Take this outside, would you please." And the pounding feet started again, only this time at least, they were heading for the back door.

Once the boys cleared the room, Katie expected Travis to pull her close again, but instead, he stepped away from her, disappearing into the kitchen. Less than a minute passed before he returned, taking Katie by the hand and heading for the front door.

Knowing that Friday would be a busy day at the bakery, Travis had decided when the boys had barreled into the dining room, to take Katie home a bit early.

However, he also knew that, as soon as they were alone together in the car, he would want to kiss her again, and there was almost nowhere in Abbott Creek that they could do so without someone they knew seeing them, so he took his time walking to the car.

Katie seemed perfectly content to walk hand in hand with him down the walk and around to the small driveway where he had parked. He held the door for her, and waited until she was settled before walking around to his side and sliding in.

There was a comfortable silence in the car as he backed out of the driveway and headed towards town. Travis enjoyed the quiet drive, looking over at Katie in the moonlight whenever he came to a stop sign or traffic light. This was one of the times he was glad that Katie wasn't one to always fill the silence with endless chatter.

The Chupp farm was only about fifteen minutes from his house, but he drove slowly, never racing the red lights or rushing through a stop. In fact, they were nearly to her house when inspiration struck and he drove past the driveway, heading out to the lake that was only a mile or so past her house.

Katie said nothing, but he thought he heard a gasp when they pulled in and saw that there were several buggies parked around the lake. Knowing she would want to keep a low profile, he was careful to pull far enough away that no one would recognize them, but not so far that anyone would get the wrong idea.

Once he had parked and set the brake, he turned to her. "I won't keep you long, Katie. I know you'll have a busy day tomorrow. . . your Fridays are always busy. I just wanted to have a few minutes alone with you."

Taking her hand in his, Travis leaned over to kiss one cheek and then the other in between words. "Every date. . . every moment I spend with you. . . is special."

When she looked up at him with her sweet smile, he added, "And I really love seeing how much my family enjoys being with you."

Putting his arms around her, he lowered his mouth to hers, his lips warm against her lips. She kissed him back, winding one of her hands through his hair.

They stayed like that for a long time, kissing and clinging to each other under the moonlight and Travis knew it was the right time to tell Katie what he had been waiting to say for some time now, something he had known, but been hesitant to say. Easing back, he looked into her eyes, his voice a bit husky when he spoke. "Katie, I love you."

She didn't even make him wait a second before she said, "I love you, too, Travis."

And then he was kissing her again. . . with a sudden passion that took his breath away. There was something about the kiss this time that was different. He couldn't identify it, but there was definitely something. It made it very difficult to stop kissing her and ease back.

"Katie, we have to stop. I don't want to take advantage of you."

"What if I don't want to stop?" And then she took the lead, kissing him with a fervor that belied her innocence. Initially, Travis was surprised, but he managed to hold onto his control. . . even when Katie wound her arms around his neck, holding him to her tightly. But when he felt her tongue brush against his lips, he jumped back, surprising her as much as himself. Quickly he opened his door and stepped out of the car.

"Travis, where are you going?" Katie leaned across his seat and called out. When he walked away from the car a bit, she opened her door and climbed out.

Travis let out a sigh and walked around the car to meet her. If she kept this behavior up, his plans to keep her neighbors from knowing what she had been doing this evening would go up in smoke.

Just like my self control if I'm not careful.

They met at the back of his car. "What's wrong, Travis? Don't you want to kiss me?" Katie sounded unsure of herself. . . and maybe even a little hurt.

He took both her hands in his, waiting until she looked up at him before he spoke. "Of course I want to kiss you. But I won't take advantage of you." He was struggling to keep his voice low, but their closeness made it a bit easier.

"You keep saying that, but you're not taking advantage of me. I want to be with you. I want to kiss you."

He took a deep breath and tried another tactic. "Katie, we agreed when we began dating that we would leave the past in the past, but you know I had a girlfriend before I met you." When she nodded, he went on. "I have enough experience to know that just now we were headed to a place we don't want to go. . . at least not yet."

"I'm not sure I know what you mean." She still sounded unsure and hurt. And though Travis wanted to do anything to keep from hurting her, he knew his message was far more important for her right now than worrying over her feelings.

Clearly, she was much too innocent to understand without him explaining. "What I mean is, we don't want to go so far that we can't stop."

Katie giggled. "That's silly. We can stop anytime we want to."

Travis struggled to keep his control. Out in the open, buggies parked only a hundred or so feet from them, it was easier, but something about her behavior from a few minutes ago had lit a fire within him, one that he was having difficulty extinguishing, so he insisted.

"No, it's not silly. There is a place where it is difficult—if not impossible—to stop. You have to remember that there are God-given desires that we are experiencing. . . and they are strong. These things are a part of who we are, and if we are not careful, the drives and instincts could overwhelm us."

"Is there something wrong with that?"

Clearly, she did not understand.

Travis looked right at her, trying to be certain that his expression told her just how serious he was being in the moment. "It's not a bad thing, at the right time. And if you were thinking a bit more clearly, you might see that.

But our bodies are trying to take over and those desires that burn within each of us make us want to keep going so much that we really can't stop ourselves once we let go of the control for more than a second." Travis realized that his heart was pounding at the thought of losing himself in loving Katie.

Clearly, he needed to make her understand before he took her home. "Please believe me, Katie. I want you, but I love you enough to want to protect you from what could happen if we aren't careful."

"I am still not sure I understand, but I trust you, so I'll do what you ask me to do." She shrugged before adding, "Are you taking me home now?"

"Yes, love, I am. And I'll walk you to the door and give you a brief goodnight kiss. . . as it should be. Now give me a hug and I'll take you home."

Travis wrapped his arms around Katie, giving her a quick hug, then moved to open the car door for her.

———— TEN ————

"Gudemariye, Katie." Freida remarked the next morning, as she waited for Katie to unlock the door. "This feels like old times, *jah?"* Katie nodded as she turned the key in the bottom lock.

A moment later Freida laughed and added, "Except that we both used to walk to work. And this morning, you came with Travis and Gwen in his car, and Thomas brought me in our buggy."

"Jah, things certainly have changed." Katie responded, thinking of everything that had

changed in both their lives over the last two years. "You won't believe the hard time Travis gave me when I told him I wanted them to drive around to the back and wait in the car while I unlocked the door so we could go in together."

Before she could say more, Freida burst into laughter! "Look!"

Katie turned to her friend, who was pointing at the bakery window. When she looked in the window, she could hardly believe what she saw.

Travis, Gwen and Thomas were inside the bakery. "They came in the back door." Freida voiced the conclusion Katie had already come to.

She walked inside and marched straight to Travis, who held up both of his hands as he backed away from her. "I know; you wanted to open the bakery like you used to do when you and Freida worked together, so I came in the back door to check it out."

Gwen and Freida were both giggling by then,

and Katie thought she might have heard a bit of masculine laughter mixed in as well as she confronted Travis.

"*Ach,* Travis, I know you are trying to help. . ." She tried to not sound as frustrated as she felt. "But everything is *allrecht.*"

"Yes, it is, and now that I know that, I will feel much better."

"You should have known that when I told you it would be." She turned away from him, more than a little annoyed to see that Freida and Thomas and Gwen were watching their exchange.

"I can remember a time when it was not all right, you know." He said the words softly, but it was not as if she could forget the event he was speaking of, especially since it had played such a large part in bringing them together.

She turned back to face him. "That is not fair and you know it, Travis Davis." She rushed on when he raised an eyebrow at her, opening his mouth. . . likely to argue. "This is a small town. Things like that do not happen every day like they do in the city. We're safe here."

"I know that, Katie." He reached up to wrap his hands gently around her arms. "And I know that you have no idea how rough it can get in the city. . . and I don't really want you to know, either." He shrugged before continuing. "But, unfortunately, small towns are no longer safe all of the time either."

When Katie started to speak, he put his finger to her lips. "Sweetheart, I know this was my idea to begin with, but when he found out about it, Andrew said it made him feel more secure. . . and that he'd like me to do it as part of my job here. He takes everyone's safety—including Amelia's—very seriously."

"So. . . opening the bakery and looking around for any trouble is your job now?" Katie looked up at him. She wanted to believe that was all there was to it, but there was something in his tone that told her there could be more.

"Yep." A tell-tale red stain was making its way from his ears to his face as he went on. "I didn't tell you. . . well, because I wanted you to feel like I was doing it because I wanted to protect you. That *is* why I started out doing it. It was just. . . when Andrew found out about it, he made it a part of my job."

Katie laughed then. He looked so much like what she imagined Bobby would if he were caught with his hand in a cookie jar. Deciding to let him off the hook, she threw her arms around him, squeezing tightly. "What matters to me is why you chose to do it at all. You are my hero, Travis."

"Aw shucks, ma'am." Travis drawled, clearly trying to sound like one of the cowboys his brothers loved watching on television, and this time when Freida burst into laughter, everyone joined in. . . even Travis.

When the laughter died down, Thomas folded his arms around his wife, speaking softly to her in between kisses. Travis took advantage of the opportunity to pull Katie close and kiss her as well. Gwen began wiping down the counters.

It was several minutes before Katie pushed away from Travis. "You need to go away now and stop distracting us." She moved over to the other happy couple and took hold of Freida's hand, pulling her toward the kitchen. "We have a lot to do, and not very much time at all."

Laughing, Travis and Thomas followed them to the kitchen. Travis even pulled at Katie's apron strings as she tried to tie them. She, in turn, grabbed for a dish towel and pretended to swat at him. He only took the opportunity to pull her close again. "I've got you now, missy!"

Pushing away, her cheeks flushed with color, Katie giggled. "Unhand me, sir. I've got bread to bake."

The two couples exploded with laughter and it was several minutes before Thomas spoke up. "She's right, Travis. We need to go and let them get to work." Then he leaned in quickly to kiss his wife on the cheek. "Now don't you be working too hard or lifting anything heavy today."

Freida smiled widely, giggling again a little. "Don't you be worrying about me, Thomas. Today is going to be fun!" She kissed him and then turned to put her own apron on, adding when she turned back, "I'm sure Katie won't let me lift anything heavy."

To which Katie nodded, adding, "Absolutely. She is not to lift anything heavier than a bowl of cobbler."

She smiled at her *freind* as Freida burst into

giggles again. "You *buwes* go get your work done and let us get to ours."

"All right. I guess that means I should go, too. Bye, Gwen." Travis shouted in the direction of his sister.

A moment later, she came through the swinging doors. "Bye, big brother."

Travis looked around at the others, before he leaned over and kissed Katie again. "I'll be back in a little while to pick up early deliveries." Katie only smiled after him as he headed for the door, Thomas right behind him.

After the guys left, Gwen headed back out to the front to set up for the day while Katie and Freida began preparations for baking.

It seemed like only a few minutes had passed before Gwen popped back into the kitchen.

"When is Bella coming in?"

"Not until lunchtime." answered Katie. "She'll watch the front while we take turns going to lunch. And Mrs. O'Neal should be coming in later today as well."

Gwen nodded. "By the way, Freida, thanks for helping me out front yesterday. What with Bella working less hours and customers buying bread and desserts or placing orders for the weekend, plus the phone ringing every few minutes with more orders, it seemed more like Friday!"

"*Jah,* and I appreciated your suggestion that I sit on one of the padded stools to take the orders." Freida remarked to Gwen. "Thomas said that I seemed more tired than usual yesterday. He didn't want me to work today, but I told him I would be fine. He worries too much."

"But would you even tell us if you needed to rest? Or if you needed to go home?" Gwen interrupted. "I know Mrs. O'Neal has been concerned for you and Bella. You both work so hard. Would you take a break or slow down if you needed to?"

"*Jah,* of course I would." Freida reassured them. "Well, I'm pretty sure I would anyway." She looked over at Gwen before going on, "Amish *maedels* are used to working hard from the time they're young. . . aren't we, Katie?" Katie nodded and Freida went on. "But I would never do anything to put my *bopli* in danger."

Katie was nodding before Freida finished. "Of course not. We know that." She put a hand over her *freind's.* "Thomas knows it, too. He is just worrying over you."

"I think it's sweet." Gwen added, with a smile.

Katie nodded her agreement. "It is sweet, and it is just the way it should be."

Gwen turned to Katie then. "OK, when are we going to talk about the party?" She sounded more than a bit impatient. "You said Mrs. O'Neal is coming in this afternoon, and I know we should wait for her, but if Bella is coming in then, too. . ." She left the question hanging and Katie smiled at her.

"I think we should talk about it now, don't you? Besides, soon you will have customers to wait on." Katie replied.

While the girls had chatted, Katie had been adding ingredients to the large, commercial mixer for nine-grain bread, a favorite of many of their customers. It didn't take long until the dough began to pull away from the hooks, so Katie changed the setting and while the mixer kneaded the dough, she had pulled out the ingredients for peanut butter cookies.

When she had finished scraping the bread dough onto the countertop, she shared her ideas with her two co-workers, while she squeezed and punched and pounded the dough.

"Tomorrow, as soon as the bakery closes, Mr. O'Neal will escort us over to the cafe, where everything will be set up and ready. Sean and Travis are helping to go around and let everyone know about the party."

"*Mamm* said she would come." Freida spoke up. "And she said Mary Zook and Maddie Mae are coming, but she didn't know of anyone else, except for your *mamm*." She turned to Katie then.

"Things have been a bit strained at my house lately. *Mamm* and I don't talk like we used to and from the way she talked, I got the feeling that she wasn't going to come. Then last night, after I had supper with Travis and his family, when he took me home, *Mamm* was waiting up for me."

"Uh oh. That doesn't sound *gut* at all." Freida sounded worried.

"Wait. What happened? Does Travis know? He didn't said anything about it when he came home." Gwen looked upset.

"Gwen, everything is fine. When your brother took me home, my *mamm* fixed us pie and *kaffe,* chatted a few minutes, then left the room. After Travis finished his pie, we said goodnight and he left." She shrugged before adding, "It was after I returned to the kitchen that *Mamm* came back downstairs and we talked. Why do you ask? Wasn't he fine when he got home?"

Gwen looked a bit sheepish then. "Well, actually I was in my room talking to someone on the phone, so I didn't see him when he got home."

"Who were you talking to so late at night?" Freida asked.

"Just a friend." The next moment she looked back at Katie. "So what else happened with your mom?"

"Well, she said Mrs. O'Neal had come out to talk to her. . . and that she had convinced her to come to the party. Then she went to talk to Thomas' *mamm*." Katie laughed. "She must be very persuasive because *Mamm* is planning to pick up Ida and Anna and they're all coming together."

"When I asked him, Thomas wasn't sure if his *Mamm* was going or not. So you're saying Mrs. O'Neal talked his *mamm* and sister-in-law into coming?" Freida looked surprised.

"That's what *Mamm* said. I hope lots of others from the community show up, and bring lots of gifts too. Bella and the baby will need help." Katie turned her attention to the dough again, separating it into bunches.

After weighing each one, she placed them into loaf pans, covered each one with a clean cloth and set them aside to give them time to rise.

"Freida, if you will begin mixing up the ingredients for snicker-doodles, I'll put the peanut butter cookies into the ovens."

"For sure, Katie. I love making snicker-doodles."

Gwen spoke up again, bringing their attention back to the party. "Okay guys, what are we fixing for the party? Do you need any help?"

Katie turned from the big, industrial ovens where the scent of peanut butter was already filling the kitchen.

"Yesterday, Freida and I made our baby shower mints; these are the ones made with cream cheese that everyone seems to love. Then we made some of the regular party mints; the ones made with butter."

"Are you making a special cake?" Gwen asked.

"Actually, I'm going to go with cupcakes. I think they work better with a crowd. We're hoping for a crowd. . . so we're going to plan for a crowd.”

“I heard that Sean and the others at the cafe are making a bunch of stuff for the party, too.”

Katie wondered at the rosy blush that appeared on Gwen's cheeks, but figured it wasn't the right time to ask questions, so she decided to ignore it for now.

“You heard right. Mr. O'Neal is providing some of the specialties they make for their afternoon teas. . . finger sandwiches with pimento cheese, tuna salad, or egg salad, plus assorted nuts, vegetable trays and cheese trays.”

“Katie, you have to take over some of your cookies! If people from the community are going to be there, they'll want your cookies too.” Gwen sounded insistent.

“I've been making extra cookies for days and freezing them. I'll just take them out of the freezer in the morning and they'll be soft and fresh by the time the party starts.”

"Wow! That's really good thinking." Gwen jumped when the timer went off.

As Katie began pulling cookies from the ovens, Gwen hurried back out front, even though it wasn't yet time to open.

"Hmm. . . that's strange. What's going on with Gwen?" Freida spoke softly, trying not to be overheard. "She usually stays to help until it's time to open."

Returning to her duties, Katie shrugged her shoulders. "I don't know. This isn't the first time she's acted a bit different. And today was the most she has talked in a long time. Usually she stays out front and hardly says a word to anyone but the customers."

"And being on the phone with a *freind* late at night. Is that normal for young, *Englischer maedels?*"

"Late-night phone calls might be, but she did seem to change the subject quickly when you asked who she was talking to so late at night." Katie stopped a moment to think back to her earlier conversation with Travis. "I hope she isn't getting mixed up with the wrong type of *freinden* at school."

"*Jah,* You and I were already out of school and working part-time at her age." Freida added. "I wonder if it is just possible that too many of the *buwes* and *maedels* get into trouble because they're kept in school longer. Peer pressure seems to be a big part of the problem."

"*Jah,* I learned everything I needed to know by the end of eighth grade. I have often thought it is foolishness to stay in school as long as the *Englischers* do."

"What more do people learn in school that is needed? Too many kids graduate from regular school and can't get jobs anyway. . . or need more training."

Katie laughed before answering. "You never

cared much for school anyway, Freida."

"Right. Once I knew my numbers and how to read and write, I was *gut*. I never cared overmuch about science and history. I just wanted to be a *frau* and *mamm*."

"And now look at you." Katie teased her.

Laughter filled the room as the two friends continued to prepare what was needed for the day ahead, as well as the special treats for the party.

ELEVEN

Saturday morning came with a flurry of excitement in the Chupp household. Even though her sweet *dochder* and her *freinden* at the bakery had been preparing for weeks, Martha knew that Katie felt there was not enough time to get everything finished before the party this afternoon.

Katie had been doing extra baking at home all week in preparation for the party, including the dozens of beautifully decorated cupcakes she had packed into several boxes that Travis would be picking up to deliver to the cafe later that morning.

Martha was still unsure why, but *Gott* had placed it on her heart to show Bella extra love and kindness, so Martha had been sewing tiny garments for the young woman since Katie had mentioned Bella's news to her.

When she had mentioned it to some of her neighbors, several of them had suggested a quilt, and between them, they had finished not one, but two quilts. One was a queen-size quilt in a beautiful, colorful fence rail pattern for Bella. The other was a baby quilt with a flower garden pattern in soft colors and extra soft material.

"Katie, hurry down. Travis is here for you." She called up to her *dochder* when his knock sounded at the back door.

"I'll be right down." Katie called a moment later.

Martha opened the door for the young man, inviting him in and explaining that Katie would be down soon. "Travis, do you have time for breakfast? Or perhaps a slice of pie?" He may have had breakfast at home, but young men, especially her own *buwes,* seemed to stay hungry.

"No, thank you, ma'am. Gwen is waiting in the car and I know Katie wants to get to work early."

At that moment, Katie came bounding down the stairs, carrying several boxes. "*Mamm,* can you bring the rest of the stuff with you?"

"*Jah,* Katie. The others will be here soon and we will go to the cafe early to help get ready."

"That is *gut.* I cannot leave the bakery until it closes and everything is readied for Monday morning. I expect we will all walk over together with Bella once we're done."

"I can come over and escort you to the cafe."

Travis offered. "I will let Andrew know that all of you will be coming over with me."

"That sounds like a *gut* plan to me. And everyone at the party will be ready to surprise Bella, right?"

"Right. Now I think we should be going. You are going to have a very busy day."

"*Jah.*" Katie turned back to Martha. "I will see you at the party, *jah?*" When Martha nodded, Katie leaned over to hug her and then she followed Travis out to his car.

Martha watched as the young man opened Katie's door for her, waited until she was seated and then closed it before going around to his own.

He is such a gut young man. Ach. If only he were Amish. She truly was impressed by his behavior toward her *dochder*. If he were a young Amish man, she would already be looking forward to a wedding in the near future. But to admit that she was *allrecht* with his not being

Amish felt as if she would be telling Katie it would be fine for her to stay in the *Englischer* world and never be baptized. Even if she were not shunned, it would be difficult on them all to lose Katie to the *Englisch* world.

Shaking off such negative thoughts, Martha turned from the window and began to clean up the few dishes that remained in the kitchen sink. She had much to do before leaving to meet Katie in town.

The day passed quickly. Travis and Sean supervised the ladies who came to decorate the main room of the cafe. The few customers who came in were seated in a small room that was usually reserved for private parties while everyone else was busy getting the main room of the cafe ready for the baby shower.

Across the street, Bella was kept busy taking orders, while Gwen was stationed behind the counter to wait on customers. Travis came in a few times and left with boxes, but since it was his job to make deliveries, Bella should not have had a thing to suspect.

Katie and Freida, with the help of Gwen, had finished all the orders on Thursday and they had been picked up or delivered already. Once the door was locked at noon, everyone pitched in and cleaned up the front room and the kitchen areas.

In no time at all, Travis came in the back door, ready to escort everyone across the street to the cafe.

When Bella stepped inside the large room, she looked thrilled to find more than half the ladies in town. The only men in the room were Mr. O'Neal, Sean, and Travis, but that made perfect sense, since most men kept their distance from something as trivial, in their opinion, as a baby shower.

Just inside the doorway, there were tables piled high with gifts, wrapped in brightly-colored paper. At the far end of the room, more tables were set up with all sorts of finger foods, desserts and a big punch bowl, one of which held several dozen cupcakes, decorated with pink, green, blue, and yellow frosting. In the middle of the room there were a dozen round tables with colorful tablecloths and party favors scattered across them.

Andrew made a show of escorting Bella to her seat. Freida sat beside her, with Gwen taking a seat on her other side, and Hannah, who had gotten off work early, sat down beside Freida. Katie sat beside her, with Travis on her other side, beside his sister.

As the other tables began to fill with friends and neighbors, Freida took the opportunity to tease Travis.

"Travis, are you going to join us? Have you ever attended a baby shower before?"

"Nope, this is my first one. . . and yep, I'm staying."

"Really?"

It was all Travis could do not to laugh at Freida's shocked expression as he took hold of Katie's hand under the table. He squeezed and winked at her, before turning back to answer her friend.

"No, silly. I'm not staying. . . but I am going to enjoy some of these delicious treats before I go. Then I'll be joining Sean in the kitchen until you need us to carry all the gifts out. Mr. O'Neal's truck is parked by the back door so we can load them all up and take them over to Mrs. Mueller's house in one trip."

"Oh good." Mrs. Mueller remarked. "I was hoping we wouldn't have to take everything out ourselves. Thank you, dear boy." She turned to the table behind her as Travis went off to gather up the treats he'd mentioned, where Cissy Davis was sitting with Martha Chupp and her daughter-in-law, Mary, who was married to Ervin, Martha's oldest son.

"You raised that boy right, Cissy. I know you've had a rough time, but you have some mighty good children that you can be proud of."

"Thank you, Ada. I don't know what I'd do without them. They are a big help to me."

Martha put her hand on top of Cissy's. "I thought I would let you know that Katie's *dat* and I have been very impressed with Travis. I don't have to tell you that we were more than a little concerned when she told us they were courting. But he has given us no reason to worry."

"That's good to know. And I want to tell you how much we enjoy having Katie over to supper on Thursdays. The kids look forward to her visit each week. . . as do I."

After everyone did justice to the sandwiches, chips, nuts, mints, cupcakes, and punch, Travis, Sean and Mr. O'Neal made themselves scarce while the ladies oohed and aahed over each and every baby gift.

Bella was sitting up front, next to the nearest table that was laden with gifts. One by one, Gwen would hand her a gift to open, while Mrs. O'Neal would write down the item and the name of the giver so Bella would have a record of who gave her each gift.

Being a small community, there had been no

gift registry, yet there were very few duplicates, unless the number of onesies, gowns, and diapers counted.

There were big gifts and small gifts. . . handmade gifts and purchased gifts. . . but Bella seemed to deeply appreciate them all. She oohed and aahed over each one with everyone else, taking her time opening the wrapping, and telling the giver how beautiful it was, or how much it was needed, or how thoughtful a gift it was.

Katie thought Bella looked shocked when the large box that held the quilts was opened. She was obviously surprised. . . and clearly overwhelmed by the beautiful handmade gifts.

Katie noticed that there was no sign of a box with all the beautiful baby clothes her *mamm* had made. She started to mention it, then decided that her *mamm* might have not brought it for some unknown reason.

Later, when all the gifts had been opened, Katie's *mamm* took her aside and in hushed tones told her that she had decided to give Bella the quilts at the party; and that she had dropped off the box of baby clothes at Mrs. Mueller's house to be opened there.

Katie recognized right away that her *mamm* was trying not to flaunt how much she had done for the young mother-to-be. Not one to outdo anyone, Martha had only done what she felt would be needed.

At that moment, Travis and Sean made their way to the front. Travis brought in a bassinet, Sean carried a baby swing, and Mr. O'Neal followed them, pushing a stroller with a matching carseat.

"Bella, these are from the employees here at the cafe. We hope you enjoy them." Andrew winked at his wife, then looked back at Bella. "And whenever you're ready to go, we'll be moving everything to Mrs. Mueller's home for you."

"Oh, Mr. O'Neal, I don't know what to say. I never expected. . ." Bella looked around at everyone, tears falling down her cheeks. "You all have done so much!"

"Nonsense, girl. You're a part of this community now and we take care of each other." Andrew looked a bit flustered, as if he was not quite comfortable around weeping females. His wife, however, knew just what was needed.

Putting her arms around the young woman, Amelia gave Bella a gentle hug and pressed a handkerchief into her hand. "We consider you a part of our family now." And she must have noticed the tired look on Bella's face, because a moment later she added, "I think you've had enough excitement for today. It's time we took you home. You need your rest."

Taking his cue from his wife, Andrew began stacking boxes. "Here, Sean. Carry these out to my truck, then come back for another load. Travis, put that bed thingie in the back of the truck and come back for the swing."

After giving everyone time to say goodbye to Bella, Amelia and Ada Mueller led her out to Amelia's car. Amelia, with a wave to Katie, Freida, and Gwen, drove off in the direction of Ada's house.

"Whew! That was a great success!" Freida exclaimed. "And it went much better than I had hoped."

"*Jah,* it was a very *gut* party. Bella should be pretty much set up for awhile." Katie looked around. "And now I think we should pitch in and help clean up this room. Gwen, why don't you fix up a box of sandwiches and goodies to take home for your family."

"That's a great idea, thanks."

Katie had noticed that Gwen had been quiet most of the time. She hoped Gwen didn't have a problem with Bella; they seemed to get along all

right at work. If she could just figure out what
was wrong. . .

TWELVE

Monday morning was a busy day at the bakery. With just three more days until the Flag Day celebration, everyone in the community was busy preparing to celebrate with family, friends, food, and fun!

Lots of special orders had come in and it was all Katie and Gwen could do to keep up with them. In the kitchen area of the bakery, Katie and Gwen flew back and forth so quickly that

Mrs. O'Neal stayed in her office so she wouldn't be in their way. Later, when Mr. O'Neal came by to ask if she wanted to accompany him on an errand, she looked relieved.

Katie was delighted to have Gwen's help. Even though Katie was still faster, Gwen had learned much during the past few months. Although she still had much more to learn, Gwen could already be counted on to do her share of the baking.

And, there was still a small chance Mrs. O'Neal would need someone to take over for her. Katie wanted to hope that her *mamm's* coming to Bella's shower, and her comments to Cissy Davis about Travis might mean that her parents had changed their minds about her quitting her job, but since they had not specifically said so, she didn't want to be overly hopeful. Which meant she was glad to have the opportunity to teach Gwen more.

It was also fortunate for Freida, who spent most of her time helping Bella with customers. Several times, when the bakery was empty, Katie had heard them chatting about baby names and all things related to pregnancy.

Mrs. O'Neal had asked Katie and Freida to watch over Bella to make sure she didn't overdo. Katie was grateful for it because it meant every hour or so, Freida would insist that Bella take a break for a few minute, and she would take a break as well.

Katie had just taken a sheet of sugar cookies out of the oven when the sound of the back door opening had her and Gwen looking up from their work.

"Hello, girls. We're back." Mrs. O'Neal came in, followed by her husband. Andrew had his arms laden with packages.

"Goodness, what did you buy?" asked Gwen, her curiosity showing on her face, as well as in her voice.

"More baby clothes." responded Andrew. "It seems that my dear wife is afraid Bella's little girl will outgrow all her clothes and have nothing to wear."

"Stop teasing me, Andrew. You had more fun picking out dresses and outfits and shoes than I did. And you are the one who insisted on not one, but two little purses for a babe who isn't even born yet." Amelia tried to sound indignant, but couldn't hide her smile.

"*Boplin* do grown up quickly." Katie commented. "It seems in no time at all they're growing out of their clothes. *Mamm* was fortunate to have clothes from previous *boplin* to use with each of us, although she usually made a few new things with each *bopli,* too." Katie smiled at the thought of the babies she had helped care for at home.

She hoped to have babies of her own someday.

"I thought as much." Amelia looked at her husband with a smile. "There's no sense in buying more newborn clothes, when the child will need bigger clothes soon enough." She looked back to Katie and Gwen then. "We bought several things in different sizes. . . since she opened gifts with 3 month size clothing, we bought clothes in six month, twelve month, and eighteen month sizes."

"And I suppose the little patent leather shoes and purse will have to wait for a couple of years."

Mrs. O'Neal laughed at the comment. "Yes, dear heart. They will."

"But I bet Bella will be glad to have them someday." Andrew commented.

"Yes, I'm sure she will enjoy them." Amelia smiled, and turned toward her office. "Let's go put these packages in a safe place for now. We don't want to overwhelm Bella with too much at once." Amelia headed towards her office. "Then I want to go out and speak to her for a few minutes before we leave."

Travis knew Katie had a lot on her mind, so he tried to be helpful and stay out of the way. This week he would be making deliveries three times a day, instead of two, so he'd have more opportunities to see her anyway.

Thursday he would be escorting Katie to the celebration and he was feeling such joy it was a wonder he could concentrate on his work at all.

Holidays are certainly a big celebration in Abbott Creek. I don't know of any other place that comes together to celebrate holidays like this community.

Like most of the community events, each family would bring enough food to feed the members of their own family, plus an extra dish or two to share. He had first discovered this practice when his family had been invited to the Independence Day celebration two years ago. Their family had not been able to bring any food, but so many other families had brought enough extra that there had been more than enough for everyone.

Since Travis had moved back to Abbott Creek from the city, the community had done much to help them out with extra food and all sorts of odd jobs. Only since his job at the cafe had become full-time had the ends truly begun to meet. Though at times there was still a need to be met.

There were still times that he would open the front door to find that something had been left on the porch. It had almost become a family joke that they had no idea who the contributors were or how they seemed to know just what was needed. Secretly, Travis thought it must be God speaking to the people. Nothing else made much sense.

Travis had even been embarrassed a few times about it, until Mr. O'Neal had met with him privately and had a heart to heart talk about it all.

He had made Travis see that giving to others was a blessing to the giver—and the receiver. To not accept a gift was hurtful to the giver, as well as denying his family of something they needed. That had made it a little easier on Travis.

He had also taken that and applied it to his own efforts. Though he worked part-time at the bakery and full-time at the cafe, he continued to work among his English and Amish neighbors, doing odd jobs and helping wherever needed.

He was a hard worker and so far, he had paid off all of his mother's medical bills and the outstanding bills left over after his father's death, plus put a little into savings. He rarely took anything for himself, except to keep his car running and for an occasional date nowadays.

Sean was busy at the Irish Blessings Cafe, learning more about bookkeeping procedures that were necessary in running a business. Travis usually sat in on the meetings. He had a head for figures and Sean appreciated having someone trustworthy who could back him up.

Why, Travis could probably cover for me if I were away for awhile. Which is a load off my mind.

When his mum had sent him to help Uncle Andrew, he had not been prepared to have the whole business dumped in his lap!

Not that I'm complaining. It's a Godsend. That's what it is. . . having my own business means I can marry sooner, rather than later.

Lately, Sean had been thinking a lot about the future—his future—with a certain lady.

If I had known when I came here, would I have refused? Or leaped at the chance? What am I supposed to do when I want her to be mine, but the chances of things working out are slim.

The whole situation was beyond frustrating. *I mean, she says she cares. . . she acts as if she does. . . but does she really know? How can she really know for sure?*

And am I the right man for her, or should I insist on giving her time to know for sure if she wants me?

At the same time, he could not stand to think of her being with someone else. Just the thought of it was too painful to bear. *I think I've loved her since the moment we met.*

What am I to do?

——— THIRTEEN ———

It all started Wednesday morning. . .

Bella and Freida had been waiting on customers all morning, when all of a sudden, Bella doubled over in pain.

"Ow!"

"Is it the baby? Is the baby coming?" Walter Grayson, who had come in to the bakery for his morning danish, rushed over to the young woman, holding out a hand to her. . . in case she needed it.

Bella flushed with embarrassment. "No, sir. It's just a cramp. Nothing to be concerned about."

"Are you sure, young lady? You don't want to be taking any chances with that baby, you know."

"Yes, sir. I'm sure. Besides, I've been getting what the book calls Braxton Hicks contractions. That's normal during these last few weeks."

"Well, all right. As long as you're certain." Walter didn't look completely convinced, but there wasn't anything else he could do about it.

After he left, Bella sat down at one of the tables for a minute.

Whew! If the doctor hadn't reassured me that I had weeks to go, I might wonder about it, too. Maybe I should mention the cramps at my appointment next Tuesday.

After resting a few minutes, she returned to

the counter, just in time for another customer.

"Gwen, what's next on the list?" Katie asked, hoping they would be able to finish today's orders soon.

"Six dozen cupcakes. . . half white and half chocolate. Two dozen with red frosting, two dozen with blue and two dozen with white." Gwen read from the clipboard holding all the customer orders to be completed on Wednesday. "Red and blue star-shaped sprinkles on the cupcakes with white frosting, and white star-shaped sprinkles on the cupcakes with red and blue frosting."

"That sounds easy enough. You want to take that one? If you do, then read me the next order and I'll start on that one."

"Sure! I love making cupcakes. . . who doesn't?" Gwen turned to start gathering ingredients, turning back when Katie cleared her throat. "Oh yeah, first I need to read off the next order, don't I?"

She turned the page on the clipboard to read the next order off to Katie. "The mayor's wife placed an order for a triple chocolate three-layer cake with milk chocolate frosting and dark chocolate shavings."

"Hmm. . . that's a new one." Katie was intrigued. The Mayor's wife almost always presented a bit of a challenge, but this cake sounded almost too simple, for her anyway.

Gwen's voice was filled with concern. . . and relief. "I'm glad you're doing her cake, instead of me. I'll get started on the cupcakes."

Katie was taking the three cake pans out of the oven when the girls heard a loud crash!

"Katie, come quick!"

Katie was shocked to hear the fear in Freida's voice. She hurried past the swinging doors to find Freida helping Bella into a chair.

"Is everyone *allrecht?* What happened?" Katie asked, not knowing what to expect. Looking down at the floor, she noticed a large wet spot. "Who spilled the water? Bella, did you slip?"

Bella was shaking her head as Gwen skidded to a stop beside them, an expression of fright and worry on her face. "Gwen, everything is *allrecht.* Please run get a mop and some floor cleaner."

"Katie, wait. That's not plain water."

"Not. . ." She looked up at her *freind.* "What is it, then?" It took a minute for Katie to realize what Freida was trying to tell her. "Is it—? I mean, did Bella's water break?"

Bella was sitting down, holding her stomach. She opened her mouth to speak, but no words came out.

"Freida, tell me what happened." Katie asked her friend.

"One minute Bella was wiping down the table. Then, when she turned to walk back to the counter, she suddenly bent over and that's when she made a puddle on the floor."

"And that's when you called for me?"

"*Jah,* I know I should be more prepared, now that I am expecting, but I got so nervous I couldn't think." Freida still looked quite uneasy.

Gwen spoke up then. "Aren't you supposed to call her doctor, or take her to the hospital?"

"Call Ada. I promised her I would call if anything happened." Bella was insistent.

"And call Mrs. O'Neal." Katie added. "She will want to know right away."

"Ask her if we should close the bakery and take Bella to the hospital. . . or what?" Freida wanted to know. She was still standing beside

Bella, wringing her hands, obviously unsure of what else she should do.

Gwen picked up the phone and dialed the number of the cafe. A moment later, she was relaying the information. Then she hung up the phone.

It seemed like only seconds later when Mrs. O'Neal flung open the door. She rushed over to Bella, followed by Sean and Travis.

"Bella, are you all right?" Amelia asked. "What can I do for you? Do you want to lie down in my office?"

"I'm fine, Mrs. O'Neal. I've been having cramps all morning, but I thought it was just false labor. You know, it's what they call Braxton-Hicks contractions." Bella looked bewildered. "But then I guess my water broke, so I think this must be the real thing." She looked over at Freida then. "Did you call Ada yet? I'm not due. It's too early."

"Now don't you fret about that."

Everyone looked around to see Ada and Mr. O'Neal walking in. It didn't seem possible that Andrew had had time to pick up Ada and bring her back to the bakery; he must have driven as fast as possible.

"But I still have several weeks to go." protested Bella. "I'm not ready—"

"Shh. Of course you are, dear girl. And you have plenty of helpers right here." Ada's voice was steady and calm, which was likely what Bella really needed at the moment. "Now, first things first. Is someone timing your contractions?"

"*Nee,* we didn't think of that yet. I think someone should call your doctor." This was from Freida.

"Wait." Ada commanded. "I remember he said to time the contractions. He also made a point of saying not to call him until they're less than five minutes apart. And he said first babies take a long time. . . and not to get in a hurry to go to the hospital."

"All right, then let's make Bella comfortable. Where should we take you, dear?" Amelia asked.

"I want to stay here. . . but I can't stay out front, especially in wet clothes." Bella wailed.

"I brought your bag with me. I have the clothes you packed for the hospital. I think there would be something that you can change into now. And I can always bring you more clothes."

"Good. Then let's go back to my office." This from Mrs. O'Neal, who still did not sound quite convinced that they should stay where they were.

——FOURTEEN——

After Bella had changed into dry clothes, with the help of Mrs. Mueller, Katie and Freida got busy with the few orders that could not wait. Gwen headed back out front to wait on customers, with strict orders to not say anything to them about Bella's current condition. Amelia knew that if customers found out about Bella being in labor, there would be pandemonium in the bakery.

However, she hadn't counted on the customers insisting on knowing why Bella wasn't working at the counter. Since Gwen wasn't comfortable with not being truthful when asked about what was going on at the moment, she tried to be vague about it, only telling them that Bella was in the kitchen.

Regardless, it wasn't long until customers were speculating on the reason why, and most everyone came to the conclusion that either there was a problem. . . or the baby was coming.

Andrew, Sean or Travis might have helped, but Amelia had sent them back over to the cafe when Ethan had called her, saying there was a crowd of people in the cafe who had apparently come from the bakery and wanted lunch.

Andrew had gone over with the two young men in case he was needed. Then, when it was obvious they could handle the crowd, he'd headed back to check on Bella and the others.

Meanwhile, in the kitchen, Katie was glad to have Freida's help. The baking for the day was done and they were putting things in order for the next day the bakery would be open, which would be Friday.

When Amelia had decided the bakery would close on Thursday, she'd called the one customer who was scheduled to pick up their order on Thursday and asked them if another day was possible. Right now Katie was rushing to get their order finished. . . and making extra cookies and treats so they could keep up with the orders the crowd that had gathered in the bakery were placing while they waited.

"Freida, I don't know what I would have done without you. Gwen is getting much better at baking, but today has been easier because you already know just what needs doing.”

“*Jah,* and it has been *gut* to have something to do while we wait.”

Katie was nodding when Freida went on. “You know I miss working with you. Thomas and I had talked about me coming back to work after the *bopli* is here, but. . .” Freida shrugged, and though Katie wanted to tell her friend that she should come back to work, she knew Freida would be much happier at home being a wife and mother.

“As much as I would love that, I know we would all understand if you don't. Your family needs you.”

“*Jah.*” was all Freida said and they both went back to work.

Katie was also keeping tabs on what was happening in Mrs. O'Neal's office. . . Bella's contractions were getting stronger and more regular. Although both Amelia and Ada kept trying to convince Bella to lie down on the couch in the office, she just kept walking back and forth, from the far wall in the office, through the kitchen to the back door, and back again, over and over.

"The doctor says walking is the best thing to help labor to progress. From what the book says, I could be lying down for hours when I reach the hospital. And I can't lie down now. I'm too nervous." Bella insisted.

While Katie checked in on Bella, Amelia went out to check on Gwen. When she pushed through the swinging doors, she could hardly believe the crowd before her.

Every single table was claimed and people

were standing in small groups all around the room as well.

"Where did all of these people come from? I thought most of them left." Amelia asked Gwen, while she rushed to fill the order she had just taken.

Gwen shrugged as she dropped cookies into a small paper bag. "I don't know. It looks to me like the same group who was here before, and then some." When Amelia handed over the bag while Gwen filled a coffee cup, she added, "Maybe the original group who went over to the cafe to have lunch, finished and came back here."

Shaking her head at the oddities of small towns, Amelia looked toward the swinging doors just as Andrew pushed them open and walked into the room. "I don't suppose we can hide this much longer." Andrew shook his head in agreement and she went on. "Would you be the one to let everyone know what is going on?"

"I can do that, darlin'."

Amelia moved over to where Gwen was taking the next order, glad to have Andrew's help in this situation. She and Gwen would take care of the customers and let him handle the crowd.

Freida hadn't said much while she was busy with the baking and cleaning, but once she was done with her work, she turned to look at Bella, who was still pacing back and forth.

"*Allrecht.* I think I have been more than patient up to now, Bella. Don't you think it's past time that you told us about the father. . . and why he hasn't shown up. . . and why he never married you?"

"Freida!" Katie was shocked that Freida would mention it now, while Bella was in labor.

Bella looked at Freida, then at Katie, and finally around to Amelia and Ada.

"Bella, you don't have to say anything. It's no one's business but yours." Amelia assured her.

"I know, but honestly, it'll probably be easier just to let them know. I'd rather tell it now and get it over with. . . I wish I could be sure that I'll never have to talk about it again, but that might be too much to hope for."

"Bella," Katie could see the distress on her face. "You really don't have to say anything. . . to anyone."

"Just let me take my time. . . but please don't let it go any farther than this room. I don't think I could stand it if everyone in town knew." She stopped then, took a deep breath, and started again. "Or maybe it would be better if people knew. Maybe what happened to me could end up helping someone else."

At that moment, the back door opened. Travis and Sean walked in, accompanied by Ethan Lewis and Lena Schrock, the local midwife.

"Hey, Lena stopped at the cafe and we told her she might be needed over here. We kicked out all the customers hanging around, then closed and locked the cafe and headed over here."

"Sean, tell me you're joking." Amelia started...

"Yeah. I'm kidding. The customers finished eating and headed back over here, so we took advantage and locked up, then headed back over, too. The bakery is full of people; I think half the town is in there."

Everyone looked at Bella when she suddenly cried out in pain.

"Honey, do you want to lie down? Why don't I check your vitals?" Lena suggested.

"No! I have to tell my story now. . . before the baby comes. I have to hurry."

"All right, if you're sure." Lena looked to Katie, but the only response was a tight nod.

"I'm sure. Travis, please go get your sister. I want her to hear this from me. Hurry!"

Katie thought she had never seen such a look of shock on his face, but he hurried past the swinging doors into the bakery. In less than a minute, he was back with Gwen in tow.

"Okay. I'm ready." Bella took a deep breath, a breath she let go in a whistle. Then she began. . .

"I grew up in a suburb just outside Chicago.

My parents have a nice home there, but when I began college, they thought it would be better for me if I lived on campus." She shrugged a little as she went on. "I thought it was a great idea. I had a nice roommate and it was much easier being close to my classes, the library, and made it easier to hang out with my friends.

One night, about six weeks after school began, I went to a freshman social. I don't drink alcohol. I never have. But I thought the party would be a great way to make new friends. When a guy came up and asked if he could buy me a drink, I politely said no. And I already had a soft drink that I was sipping on.

After he walked away, I went to the ladies room. When I came back, I finished my soda and looked around for someone to talk to. It wasn't too long until I started to feel strange. . . very strange. . . dizzy.

Since I had only been drinking soda, I figured

it was because the room was so warm, so I told my new friends I was going back to my dorm room and I left. I vaguely remember leaving, but I don't remember anything else until I woke up the next morning—alone—in the back seat of a car. I didn't even know whose car it was, or how I got there.

I couldn't really remember anything. I felt like I had woken up from a nightmare, but the images in my head were fuzzy and jumbled. Nothing really made sense. And the more I thought about it, the more I worried that it might not have been a nightmare, but something that had happened to me, and I freaked!

I grabbed my stuff and ran back to my room. Thankfully, my roommate had already left for class. I took a long shower and put on my pajamas and went to bed. I cried and cried, because I knew somehow that something terrible had happened to me. I didn't tell anyone; I just *kept it all to myself.*

Three weeks later, I missed my period. It was pretty easy by then to figure out what had happened.

I withdrew from school, went home and told my mom I needed a break. She could see that something was wrong, but since I refused to talk about it, she had no idea what had happened.

When both my parents kept after me to explain what was going on and why I had left school, I packed my things and left.

I drove and drove, until I stopped here for coffee, and to use the ladies room. The first person I ran into was Mrs. Mueller. She was so sweet. I guess she could see that something was wrong. Then she did the strangest thing. . . she asked if I needed a place to stay. And somehow I knew this would be a safe place, so I said yes. She didn't ask any questions; just took me back to her house and helped me settle into a room.

It was she who suggested I apply for a job here at the bakery. And honestly, the longer I stay, the more I love this town.

I never, ever want to live in a big city again, or even near one. I don't ever want to go anywhere you can get drugged and bad things can happen to you. I just want to stay here and raise my baby. It's not her fault that this happened to me. When I met my parents in January, I told them what happened. They were furious that I didn't tell them sooner, and that I had left home.

They kept talking about me giving up the baby and going back to college. I can tell you right now, that is never going to happen. I'm never going back there. And I'm not giving up my baby, either. She's the only good thing to come out of this mess.

And as much as I hate thinking of what must have happened, and the result of it, I will do anything to make sure nothing like that ever happens to any of the girls who live in this community.

I'm especially concerned about the Amish and Mennonite girls. How would they ever suspect that such evil exists? I would hate for anything like that to happen to you, Katie. . . or you, Gwen."

No one had moved while Bella was sharing her story. When she was done, there were tears in the eyes of everyone in the room.

Mr. O'Neal was the first one to speak. "I am so sorry that such a horrible thing happened to you. We'll do anything we can to help you. . . and to make you feel safe."

"Thank you, sir. Your wife has been

awesome. I—" Bella cried out, doubled over in pain.

Quickly, Lena was at her side. "I think it's time we get you to the hospital, unless you want to have this baby right here!"

"No! No hospital!" Bella's words were said through clenched teeth, accompanied by her pushing away from the people who had all reached out to help her.

"Bella, dear, you cannot have the baby here. It's not safe or sanitary." Lena's words were very calm, but Bella insisted.

"I am not going to the hospital."

Freida spoke up then. "Is there something wrong with the hospital?"

"No. . . city. . ." Bella said each word with a hard expulsion of breath.

"*Allrecht,* we will not go to the hospital." Lena reassured the young woman while motioning to Katie to come and help her. "You need to let me check you out. It will tell us how much time we have, at least.”

“O. . . K. . . Just no hospital.”

“I promise.” And with that, Lena led her away to the small office Amelia used at the bakery.

It was no more than five minutes when Lena came rushing out of the office. “We have to get her somewhere now. The baby is so close, we wouldn't have time for the hospital anyway.”

Freida spoke up then. “If she won't go to the hospital, would she go to your house?”

Katie was nodding before Freida finished speaking. Hearing a cry, Lena went back into Mrs. O'Neal's office.

“On second thought, there's no time for that, either.” Lena said, coming back to the door. “Ada, your house is closest.”

“Yes, that's fine. Let's just get her there.”

Amelia and Ada rushed into the office to help

Bella walk outside to Andrew's truck, which he had quickly pulled around to the back door.

—— EPILOGUE ——

The sun was shining on Flag Day, assuring the town of a glorious day. Everyone would be gathering in the square in a few hours to celebrate.

Katie and Travis would be arriving together. Katie's family would be attending along with the rest of the community. Mr. O'Neal had arranged for John Baker to pick up the rest of the Davis family and bring them to the square.

Andrew and Amelia were picking up Ada Mueller, along with Bella and her beautiful, newborn daughter, Emma, who would no doubt get more than her share of attention.

The day before, Travis had driven Katie and his sister to Ada's house to help with the birth, and they had arrived with only minutes to spare. In addition to Ada and Amelia, Bella had requested that Katie, Gwen, and Freida stay with her. It had been a bit crowded at times, but none of them would ever forget the experience.

Ada had told Bella she should stay home and rest, but Bella had assured her that she was well enough to be at the Flag Day celebration.

She had given Katie permission to share her story with her parents, in hopes that sharing her experience might help to keep Katie's younger *schweschders* safe.

The next morning, her parents had surprised her when they told her they had accepted her decision to not join the church. . . and that Travis was a fine, young man and they were glad that she had found someone who would treat her with respect.

Then they had suggested that Katie ask Travis to come to the Chupp home once a week for supper so the family could get to know him better. Martha had also suggested that Travis' family come to supper on a regular basis.

Katie had been too shocked to say anything, but they hadn't really looked as if they'd expected a reply. A moment later, Katie's *dat* had told her that Travis was there to pick her up, and her *mamm* had gathered Katie in a hug and reminded her the family would meet her and Travis later at the celebration.

Katie still wasn't sure why her parents had had such an unexpected change of heart, but whatever the reason was, she was thrilled to know that she could pursue a relationship with

Travis, without having to move away from her family.

Remembering that Travis was waiting for her, Katie quickly gathered what she wanted to take and headed outside to meet her boyfriend.

Katie couldn't wait to share the gut news with him!

RECIPES

Katie's Peach Cobbler

Katie's Baby Shower Mints

Katie's Party Mints

Gwen's Baby Shower Cupcakes

Katie's Peach Punch

Peanut Butter Krispie Treats

Katie's Rice Pudding

Martha's Cooked Apples

Naomi's 7 Layer Salad

Naomi's Honey Mustard

Naomi's Garlic Herb Spread

Amish Wedding Broccoli Cheese Soup

KATIE'S PEACH COBBLER

INGREDIENTS:

1 cup self-rising flour

1 cup white sugar

2 cups peaches, sliced

1/2 cup unsalted butter

1 large egg

1 teaspoon pure vanilla extract

INSTRUCTIONS:

Preheat oven to 350F. Grease 2qt baking dish with butter. Spread sliced peaches in baking dish. Sprinkle 1/2 tablespoon sugar over top of peaches.

Blend remaining sugar and softened butter until mixed well. Add flour to mixture. Add egg and vanilla extract. Mix well. Spread batter over tops of peaches.

Bake for 35-40 minutes, until crust is brown. Let stand 10 minutes before serving. Best served with ice cream.

Yield: Serves 12 *(or 2 expectant mothers)*.

KATIE'S BABY SHOWER MINTS

INGREDIENTS:

8 ounces cream cheese, softened

1/2 cup unsalted butter, softened

2 1/2 cups confectioners sugar

1 teaspoon pure mint extract

2-3 drops pink food coloring

2-3 drops blue food coloring

2-3 drops green food coloring

2-3 drops yellow food coloring

Mix together cream cheese and butter. Add 1 cup of the confectioners sugar. Stir until mixed well. Add mint extract and stir to mix well. Slowly add another cup of confectioners sugar, mixing until smooth and creamy. To make 4 multiple colors, separate dough into 4 bowls. Add 2-3 drops of food coloring to each bowl and mix until desired color. Cover. Refrigerate for several hours.

Line two cookie sheets with wax paper and dust with confectioners sugar. Form dough into 1â€‍ balls and roll in the confectioners sugar. Flatten each ball with the tines of a fork. Let stand, uncovered until mints are firm (this will take several hours). Store in airtight container (with wax paper between layers).

Yield: 8 dozen.

KATIE'S PARTY MINTS

INGREDIENTS:

1 cup unsalted butter, softened

32 ounces confectioners sugar

2 tablespoons whole milk

2 teaspoon pure vanilla extract

1 teaspoon pure mint extract

2-3 drops pink food coloring

2-3 drops blue food coloring

2-3 drops green food coloring

2-3 drops yellow food coloring

Mix butter and 1 cup confectioners sugar until

smooth and creamy. Gradually add remainder of sugar, blending well. Add milk, vanilla extract and mint extract. To make 4 multiple colors, separate dough into 4 bowls. Add 2-3 drops of food coloring to each bowl and mix until desired color.

Line 2 cookie sheets with wax paper. Form dough into 1" balls; place on pan. Flatten each ball with the tines of a fork. Refrigerate until ready to serve.

Yield: 8 dozen

GWEN'S BABY SHOWER CUPCAKES

CAKE:

2 cups cake flour

1 tablespoon baking powder

1/2 teaspoon salt

1 cup white sugar

3 large egg whites

1 cup heavy cream

1/2 cup cold water

1 tablespoon pure vanilla extract

ICING:

2 cups confectioners sugar

1/2 teaspoon pure almond extract

4-6 tablespoon whole milk

* additional milk as needed

Mix together flour, baking powder, salt and sugar. Using mixer, beat egg whites until slightly stiff. Using mixer, pour cream into another bowl and beat until stiff. Add egg whites and fold together until blended. Stir water and vanilla extract together. Add to cream/egg mixture, gently stirring until blended. Gradually sprinkle onto flour mixture and stir until well blended.

Spoon batter into paper baking cups, filling each cup half full. Bake at 350F about 15 minutes or until done. Remove from oven and cool. Prepare icing, mixing confectioners sugar with pure almond extract. Add small amounts of milk until icing is desired consistency. Spread over top of cooled cupcake.

Yield: 48 cupcakes.

KATIE'S PEACH PUNCH

INGREDIENTS:

16 ounces frozen peaches

3 fresh peaches

64 ounces peach/white grape juice

2 liters sprite, chilled

1 fresh lemon

1/2 cup white sugar

6 scoops vanilla ice cream

Puree peaches until smooth. Set aside. Add sugar, gelatin and water to saucepan. Bring to boil. Stir until gelatin and sugar dissolve.

Puree frozen peaches, sugar and juice from lemon. Set aside. Pour white grape/peach juice into large punch bowl. Add pureed mixture. Slowly add chilled liter of sprite. Stir well.

Garnish with fresh peach slices.

Yield: Serves 12.

PEANUT BUTTER KRISPIE TREATS

INGREDIENTS:

3 tablespoons butter

4 cups miniature marshmallows

6 cups rice cereal

1/2 cup creamy peanut butter

Melt butter in large saucepan over low heat. Add marshmallows and stir until completely melted. Add peanut butter and stir until mixed well. Remove from heat.

Add rice cereal. Stir until well coated. Grease 9x13 baking pan with butter. Using buttered spatula, press mixture into baking pan. When cool, cut into 2 inch squares.

KATIE'S RICE PUDDING

INGREDIENTS:

1 cup whole milk

1 cup water

1 cup rice, uncooked

2 large eggs

1 cup evaporated milk

1 teaspoon pure vanilla extract

1/4 cup white sugar

1/8 teaspoon ground cinnamon

INSTRUCTIONS:

Using a 2-quart saucepan, heat milk and water

over medium heat. Add rice and bring to boil.
Lower the heat, stirring every 10 minutes. Cook
uncovered for 30 minutes, or until rice is tender.
In a large bowl, combine eggs, 3/4 cup of the
evaporated milk, vanilla and sugar. Set aside.

Add the remaining evaporated milk to the rice
mixture. Spoon 1 cup of the rice mixture into the
egg mixture and stir. Pour the egg/rice mixture
into the remaining rice. Heat until it boils, stirring
constantly. Remove from heat. Sprinkle with
cinnamon.

MARTHA'S COOKED APPLES

INGREDIENTS:

5 medium apples

1 tablespoon fresh lemon juice

1/4 cup unsalted butter

3/4 cup brown sugar

3/4 teaspoon ground cinnamon

1/4 teaspoon salt

* dash ground nutmeg

Peel and slice apples. Using a large skillet, combine apples and lemon juice on medium heat. Add butter, brown sugar, cinnamon, salt, and nutmeg. Stir, cover, and cook for 30 minutes or until apples slices are soft.

NAOMI'S 7-LAYER SALAD

INGREDIENTS:

1/2 head of lettuce

6 hard-boiled eggs

1 small onion

1 can of baby peas

2 cups mayonnaise

2 cups cheddar cheese, shredded

1 pound of bacon

Finely chop onion and saute in butter. Fry bacon, drain, and crush.

Add each ingredient, making individual layers in a large glass bowl.

Layer 1: tear up lettuce and place in bottom of bowl.

Layer 2: chop up hard-boiled eggs.

Layer 3: spread onion over eggs.

Layer 4: drain peas and add to bowl.

Layer 5: Gently spread mayonnaise over peas.

Layer 6: Sprinkle shredded cheese over mayonnaise.

When ready to serve, add layer 7: Sprinkle bacon bits over cheese.

NAOMI'S HONEY MUSTARD

INGREDIENTS:

1/4 cup mayonnaise

1 tablespoon mustard

1 tablespoon pure honey

1/2 tablespoon lemon juice

Combine ingredients and whip until well blended.

NAOMI'S GARLIC HERB SPREAD

INGREDIENTS:

8 ounces cream cheese, softened

1/4 cup parmesan

1/4 cup mayonnaise

1-2 garlic cloves

1 teaspoon Italian seasoning

1 tablespoon parsley

Combine ingredients and whip until well blended.

AMISH WEDDING BROCCOLI CHEESE SOUP

INGREDIENTS:

7 pounds broccoli, chopped

2 pounds Velveeta cheese

1 quart sweet whipping cream

1/2 cup cornstarch

* cold water

Cook broccoli, adding enough water just to cover it. When broccoli is tender, add Velvet cheese and whipping cream. Stir until cheese is melted and ingredients are mixed. Add corn starch to thicken.

TURN THE PAGE

FOR EXCLUSIVE

BONUS CONTENT

DISCUSSION QUESTIONS

WARNING : SPOILERS AHEAD!

1) Katie and Travis have decided to begin dating. . . do you think either one is putting the relationship ahead of their religious beliefs?

2) If the church were to shun Katie, she would lose contact with her family and friends. . . is her relationship with Travis worth it?

3) Do you think Katie is being truthful with herself when she says her relationship with Travis has nothing to do with her joining – or not joining – the Amish church she has always attended?

4) Bella has been keeping secrets. . . what do you think her friends will do when they find out about her past?

5) Do you think Bella did anything that could have contributed to her attack? Do you think the attacker was the man who offered to buy her a drink. . . or someone else?

6) Do you feel that Bella should have told her parents

the whole story about what happened to her? Would they have understood her reasons for leaving school?

7) Do you think she was right in keeping the baby? Or should she have followed her parents' advice and given the baby up for adoption?

ACKNOWLEDGMENTS

To God be the glory! HE is THE AUTHOR of my life! God gives me the inspiration for each and every book... books of family, faith, forgiveness, and grace...

When God placed it on my heart to write a light-hearted mystery series, I'm glad I obeyed... And when HE kept after me to write about a serious occurrence happening not only on school campuses, but in unexpected places, too, I struggled with it, but with lots of prayers and tears, it's finally done.

Thanks to Rachel, who not only designs my covers, memes, posters (well, you get the picture), but is also an amazing author and inspirational speaker.

Rachel, I couldn't have done it without you!

A big thank you goes out to Pam, a dear friend and an awesome cheerleader. Thank you, Pam, for always inspiring me to never give up!

Last, but by no means least, thank you to my awesome readers, who do so much to encourage me and continue to make this series a huge success!

ABOUT THE AUTHOR

Naomi Miller mixes up a batch of intrigue, sprinkled with Amish, Mennonite, and English characters, adding a pinch of mystery, and a dash of romance!

Naomi's days are spent focusing on her writing, editing and homeschooling her grandchildren. She loves her new career as an author, blogger and inspirational speaker.

She schedules several book events each year and enjoys the opportunity to meet readers face-to-face. When she's not rushing to meet a deadline, Naomi loves to make time to attend writing conferences, workshops, and other author events.

She is a member of the American Christian Fiction Writers organization (ACFW), the Knoxville and the Authors Guild of Tennessee (AGT).

Whenever time permits, Naomi can be found in one of two favorite places. . . the beach and the mountains.

Naomi loves traveling with her family, singing inspirational/gospel music, taking daily walks, and witnessing to others of the amazing grace of Jesus Christ.

AUTHOR LINKS

WEBSITE: https://naomimillerauthor.com
NEWSLETTER SIGN UP: http://eepurl.com/bPdjGn
FACEBOOK:
https://www.facebook.com/NaomiMillerAuthor
INSTAGRAM: https://twitter.com/AuthorNaomi
PINTEREST: http://www.pinterest.com/authornaomi
GOODREADS:
https://www.goodreads.com/NaomiMiller
BOOKBUB:
https://www.bookbub.com/authors/naomi-miller
INDIEBOUND: http://bit.ly/1PsB9MR
FICTION FINDER: http://bit.ly/1UOlI5P

MORE FROM

S&G PUBLISHING